The Secret of the Dragon
The Revelations of the Sacred Papyruses

Carl Cupper

ISBN: 1-4196-1757-5
Library of Congress Control Number: 2005909385
Publisher: BookSurge, LLC
North Charleston, South Carolina

To order additional copies, please contact us.
BookSurge, LLC
www.booksurge.com
1-866-308-6235
orders@booksurge.com

Original title:
El Secreto del Dragón – La Revelación de los Sacros Papiros
Translation by: John Alden Boyd, Jr.

Cover illustration, "Golden Dragon" by:
Ciruelo Cabral
www.dac-editions.com

Editorial design by:
Editorial Perfiles 23
Av. Circunvalación Poniente # 7
Naucalpan Edo. de México C.P. 53240.
Tel. (55) 56-87-75-57, (55) 53-73-93-57
razo@avantel.net

To the young people of the world
who grasp a weapon without knowing why

The Region of Fire

Arbux

Farox

Rhusux

Amerux

Anglox

Atlantix
Ocean

ISUX

Atlantix
Ocean

Helenex

★ Dragonia

The Court of Helenex

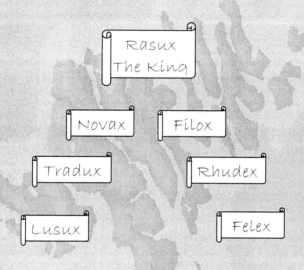

Rasux
The King

Novax

Filox

Tradux

Rhudex

Lusux

Felex

Linage of Califax

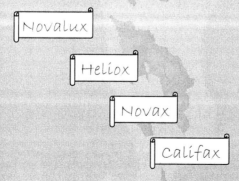

Novalux

Heliox

Novax

Califax

Introduction

July 1191
Jerusalem

ISAIAH HURRIEDLY PACKED THE LARGE NUMBER OF documents collected over the last millennium by the school of the Flavius Josephus, a prominent Jewish historian.

The alarming news that the city of Acre had been hit spread all over Palestine, the historian had a growing fear. The killings that Richard I, the Lion-Heart, had inflicted on that city meant that he could not delay. Richard's crusaders had defeated the Muslims of Saladin and would soon be at the doors of Jerusalem, the objective being to recuperate the sacred city in the name of Jesus Christ. Jacob, a disciple of Isaiah, had tried in vain to convince his teacher not to abandon Jerusalem, but Isaiah, knew the hearts of men, moreover, the cruelty of Richard, and he would not risk his life, nor the valuable documents collected for the academy throughout the years.

Years ago, Isaiah ventured out on a journey to Qumran where he had hid many valuable documents before, but he still had many more documents that he needed to protect with his life. And so, he would make a secret expedition to Egypt, where he thought he could find a safe refuge for his valuable papyruses. Jacob, only, would be trusted with the knowledge of this risky expedition, for which he was urged to carefully guard the secret.

Isaiah then undertook his bold passage. After crossing the Red Sea, he reached the village of Naj Hammadi, where he hid many more scrolls. From there, he headed south and crossed the Nile, to the city of Tebas, in the Valley of the Kings, where he was caught by surprise by a ferocious and terrifying sand storm.

Isaiah had a fierce battle against the forces of nature, that he was, undoubtedly, destined to lose. Feeling that his strength was lost, he made his way up some stairs to what looked like the entrance of a tomb. He then hid the last of the scrolls in a vase, and placed it inside the threshold, but he did not want to cover himself in that shelter, because he was afraid that the hiding place of the precious documents might otherwise be found.

Trying to find some refuge, he continued through wave of the desert sand, but the elements and intense thirst took his life under the relentless desert sun. Though it cost him his life, he achieved his mission to keep the documents from the hands of Richard and his Crusaders … at least for the following seven centuries.

1

The Mystery of the Prophecy

February 17th, 1923
Tebas, Egypt

AFTER SEVERAL ARDUOUS AND LABORIOUS DAYS OF excavations, the British archeologists, George Edward Stanhope and Howard Carter, opened the tomb of the controversial Pharaoh Tutankhamen[1], whose discovery a year ago had astonished the entire world. The tomb of the king of the XVIII dynasty was discovered intact. The tenacious and exited archeologists were so happy about the important find that their hearts almost jumped out of their chests. Huge amounts of

---

[1] Son in law to Amenhotep IV or Akhenaton, restored worship of Aton as the only god, which was probable the reason he died at the hands of his opponents. (Doctors note).

treasure were found in the tomb of the young Pharaoh. The magnificent collection of Egyptian art made of gold, ceramic, lapis lazuli, precious wood and other materials encompassed the mortuary chamber.

Later, many of the valuable objects were taken to the Ancient Museum of Egypt, in Cairo, and others to the British Museum of London, where papyruses with strange characteristics were found inside a vase. Later carbon 14 dating tests were performed on the vase: the scrolls were dated at VII century from our time. An incredible story was written on the papyruses that had been stored in some neglected container in the museum until recent times.

Victim of the terrible prophecies of the tomb of Tutankhamen, George Edward Stanhope, count of Carnarvon, died two months after his fabulous find.

March 12th, 2005
British Museum of London, England

Looking for information to complete his studies on the origins of the people of the British Isles, a prestigious doctor of History, long after graduating from the University of Oxford, found himself with those mysterious papyruses. After analyzing them, he wrote a rough draft that narrates a fabulous legend that starts with this caveat:

Many thought that this story never happened in the dark ages of the VII century or any other time. However, I have reasons to believe that it is true, and it is my duty to warn man of his uncertain destiny. This is the story as it has been divulged to me, and I tell it in order to spread the hope that resides in this tale.

In the year 306 of our era, Constantine the First moved the capital of the Roman Empire to Byzantine, and called it Constantinople, and in 313 the Edict of Milan was promulgated. In 395, Theodosius the First divided the Empire between his two sons: Arcadius received the eastern part and Honorius the west. The last of the empire disappearing in the year 476, a half of a century after the Christianizing of the Celtic people had begun. [2]

In the middle of the VI century, Justinian's troops from the Byzantine Emperor of the Orient conquered the Kingdom of Theodoric the Ostrogoth. Most of Italy was turned into an exarchate with its capital in Ravenna. In the year 586 of our era, the Lombards, another barbarian nation, took control of the northern portion of Italy, which was ferociously defended by the Byzantines, who, in spite of their efforts, had only managed to rescue a few coastal regions of the country. In the middle of the clash between the Lombard's and the Byzantines, the Pope of Rome tried to maintain a precarious balance while his power grew, gradually, and restored an important political and military force.

On the other hand, the Visigothic monarchy reached its maximum dominion with the Leovigild emperor, who managed to establish territorial units after winning over the Suebi of the northwest, the Basques of the north and the Byzantines of the Southeast.

---

[2] Started by Saint Patrick in 423 A.C. (Doctors note).

The invasion of the south of Great Brittan by the Anglos and the Saxons,[3] after the attacks of the Picts[4] and the Caledonians, obligated the Celts to take refuge in the highlands of Wales and Scotland where they came into power again. Many Celts directed by Maeloc, a celebrated druid bishop, went north of Galicia fleeing from the Anglo-Saxons, but others stayed on the island to conserve their sacred ancestral rites and traditions, even under siege of the invaders and the incipient Christian evangelism.

The Anglo-Saxons divided the territory into seven small independent kingdoms. Each kingdom fought to establish its dominion of the island; however, neither of their borders had touched a remote area known by all as *The Region of Fire*, which was formed by the group of Faroe Islands, located beyond the Shetland Islands, north of Great Brittan. On these islands lived two tribes that for many centuries had disputed, in bloody battles, the dominion of the *Sacred City*. The Helenex, that adored the Helion god, occupied a large portion of the territory maintaining dominance of the Sacred City. The Helenex conquered the Selenex tribe, who worshiped Selion god [5] and lived as refugees, on their own land, lacking recognition by the Helenex as an independent nation.

---

[3] In the beginning, the Celts, also known as the Gauls, asked for help from the Anglos and the Saxons (Germanic people from Anglia and Saxony regions) against the Picts and the Caledonians. (Doctors note).

[4] The Celts of the south called them *prytain* and those from Ireland, *cruthni*. Both originating in the root word *Britannia*. Other Celt tribes also called them Picts, which means, painted people. This word is probable derived from the Iron Age people that used Indigo blue in their rituals and battles. (Doctors note).

[5] Helion was the God of the Sun and Selion of the Moon. (Doctors Note).

Rasux, King of the Helenex, tried to reestablish peace with Palex, King of the Selenex, offering to withdrawal his troops from occupied territories in exchange for ceasing attacks, but without granting any part of the Sacred City, an offer that was refused.

Despite his efforts to restore communications, Palex had not been able to restrain his citizens who, inflamed by ancestral hatred, acted on their own against the Helenex, preventing between these tow tribes.

The continual attacks of the Selenex on Helenex territory, spread terror and uncertainty among its inhabitants, giving them reasons to retaliate against the High Chiefs of Selenex, particularly Palex, whom they accused of inciting great destruction and violence while he offering words of peace.

The majority of neighboring island nations sympathized with the Selenex cause, and tried to reach a peaceful agreement in the High Courts; however, their efforts were half-hearted as each benefited from the conflict by selling arms and equipment or by taking a stance that placed them in a favorable political position in the eyes of the other nations.

Occupation of Selenex territory by the Helenex would extend for a long period until one of them surrendered or destroyed the other, although, the most probable outcome of the conflagration, would be the destruction of both tribes.

These conflicts have been recurrent all through the history of humanity; however, I should clarify to the reader that the tribes in this story were in the shape of enormous and ferocious dragons.

There were three types of dragon in the *Region of Fire*. The *Robuxes,* gigantic, strong dragons of brown or dark green color, whose wings were so short that they could not fly: the reason why they were used as frightful armored dragon soldiers in the infantry.

The *Agilux* were small dragons with large wings that allowed them to fly at high altitudes and to cover long distances. They were used as sentries, explorers or as artillery dragons; the aerial combat dragons. There were two types of *Agilux*: litmus blue and pearl white.

The most ideal of dragons were the *Pantesux*. The *Pantesux* were strong dragons with large wings. They could carry out missions on land or in the air, and they were part of the elite army of the Royal Council. Their principal characteristic was that they could change color at will. They could be seen in a dark green, litmus blue, pearl white, red or grey color, depending on the circumstances they confronted in battle. These types of dragons were related to the Novax.

"For Dragonia, the Sacred City!" Novax, the Great Helenex Dragon, gave the order to attack.

The obstreperous sound of the beating of wings from the soldiers, sounded like a wasp's nest with thundering reverberations. The fire that spewed from their enormous snouts, smoldered in the air making it almost impossible to breath, and the uproar of the blows that they inflicted on one another with their powerful tails resonated, shaking the stratosphere of the region.

A squadron of powerful Helenex armored dragons, burst in into the enemy front looking for the guilty ones responsible for the most recent attacks on Dragonia.

There was much wailing and cries of pain that could be heard mixed with the sound of the sizzling flames and the clamor and destruction of the Selenex caves.

The Helenex dominated the beaches where the marine shells were steadily incoming. Luckily, they held exclusive rights to the production of the protective armor, made from the ammonite shells covered in bronze. Their protective armor covered from the eyes to the tip of the tail, making them almost invulnerable to hostile flames.

Given the enormous weight of the armored dragon's protection, their missions were more appropriate for land battle. They could invade on almost any terrain, and nothing could stop them. They relentlessly destroyed and carbonized everything in their path; thereby, inflicting terrible losses to enemy supporter's.

The dragon artillery had a device on the end of their tails made of leather and filled with sharp arrows covered with tar, which they launch at the enemy army inflicting serious damage.

Once the sharp arrows hit their unfortunate target, the dragon artillery spewed fire, incinerating the victims on contact. When the victim felt the scorching fire on their backs, they tried to put it out by rolling around on the ground; sending the sharp arrows deeper into their bodies to cause an extremely slow and painful death.

The Selenex had implemented a tactic to stop the armored Helenex. They deep holes and filled them with well-camouflaged muddy water that they distributed, strategically, around certain parts of the battlefield that they were defending. When an armored dragon fell in one of these pits, it was almost impossible for them to get out: the enormous weight of the armor that the unlucky dragon carried, causing irremediable death by drowning. The Selenex counterattacked with dragons outfitted with catapults. They carried a trowel with enormous rocks on their tail and they launched them at the enemy army. They also found a way to counteract the attacks from the armored Helenex. In order to do this they looked for a way to ignite the cargo carried on the Helenex dragon tails before it was launched. To achieve this, they sent Agilux dragons called *hunters*, who were lighter and faster than the others, because they carried no load. When the fire of a hunter knocked out the artillery, the deadly cargo exploded destroying the tail of the artillery dragon, despite its protective armor. They fell from the sky a shooting star and made long, loud reverberating sounds as they hit the ground.

Amerux, the most powerful of the tribes in the region, was selling tar on an exclusive basis to Helenex allies. Since the Selenex did not have this technology, they were restricted to lighting the artillery dragon's tail on fire in battle. They also went on suicide missions to destroy the enemies' warehouses during truce, something that happened often even though these weapons warehouses were carefully guarded by an elite group of enormous and ferocious Pantesux dragons.

After several hours of cruel battle, the moans and cries of the wounded became unbearable to the noble ears, and the dragons who were not hurt, rested and picked up their mutilated soldiers and to bury their dead.

After that catastrophe, on the eve of that unlucky day, Califax, son of Novax, was born along with two brothers and two sisters.

The light of new life came to the world. The proud parents notified the inhabitants of the nation, who had congregated in large numbers for the event. They celebrated by drinking barley liquor, and happily lit the sky with enormous flames originating from deep within their entrails.

While Darta, Califax's sweet and beautiful mother warmly sang the newly born to sleep, Novax uselessly tried to contain the roars of joy that burst from his friends outside the comfortable cave of the flamboyant happy parents.

"¡Hey, Novax! Now you will know what the real warmth of home feels like, friend," said Felex with an enormous, mocking laugh.

"Silence, please! Lower the volume of your grumbling!" Novax pleaded, putting a claw to his snout. "The pups are sleeping and my wife is tired, my friends," he explained, murmuring, while he made a gesture with his claws.

"You should sleep too, my friend, while you still can," Rhudex advised. "Later, you will get white scales from the insomnia and other things," he said, provoking the widespread laugh of the concourse.

"Silence, dragons!" reprimanded Gramma, Felex's wife. "Can't you see that the pups have just broken their eggshells? They need their rest after such a traumatic event," she complained her husband throwing him a ferociously stern look.

The dragons looked at one another with wide eyes of surprise, and, shamefully, lowered their heads and immediately took their leave under the rigorous examining eyes of Gramma who, claws on hips, followed the sluggish steps of her husband.

"Tomorrow we meet in the assembly, Novax," said Rhudex, mumbling.

"Very well, my friend. Thank you very much for visiting!" he expressed to the rest of the dragons who silently walked away.

Inside the cave, Novax sat with his wife and the small offspring. The day had been long and he too felt tired, as he fell into the rock bed that was covered in a comfortable and cool mould.

"Do you think we will be safe from the Selenex, my love?" asked Darta, concerned.

"Yes dear. Even though they are becoming more fierce and cruel," he said, lying down heavily on the rock. "Nevertheless, as long as we have warriors like Rhudex, we will be safe. I hate the fact that our children have been born in the middle of all this hostility!" she complained, covering her face with her claws.

"Calm down my love," he said, caressing his wife's forehead. "Someday all this will be over."

The night's dark cloak enveloped the area in a false calm, like in the eye of a hurricane, but crowding around the homes, the war had settled like a demon which claims his ancient lodgings to anyone dares to profane them.

The next day, the assembly of the Royal Dragon Council gathered to discuss policy and strategy regarding the conflict with the Selenex. There were reports of the tally of wounded, dead, and the extent of the destruction. Most importantly, the main enriched tar warehouse had sustained substantial damage.

Rhudex made a proposal to exterminate the Selenex once and for all. His idea that was rejected immediately by the Council for fear the League of Dragons would severely retaliate against them. In answer to that refusal, Rhudex proposed that some other member of the League surrender their land to the Selenex; "If they have so much consideration towards the Selenex!" he said, full of rage.

Rasux explained that the Selenex would not in give up Dragonia for anything, since it was also sacred ground to them.

Novax, a dragon of great restraint and wisdom, suggested and proposed to consider giving a part of the Sacred City to the Selenex. But Tradux, indignant at such a preposterous proposal furiously reminded him that the Sacred City was constructed with the very fire and blood of the one and only Helion god, after his ancestors were released from the oppression that they were subjected to for many centuries.

"We should raise our walls even more!" he suggested angrily, jumping out of his seat as if a catapult propelled him.

Novax refuted the arguments of Tradux with great patience and serenity.

"Perhaps Helion would allow us to yield a part of Dragonia, in exchange for living in peace," said Novax, in a conciliatory tone.

The voices of the members of the council were enraged at the profane proposal. Some seriously considered Novax's argument, but others yielded and supported Tradux's idea. King Rasux indicated that, the idea had crossed his mind frequently, because of the terrible death toll that both nations had suffered. However, Lusux, another distinguished dragon of the court, indicated that the constant suicide attacks prevented establishing any kind of dialogue that would lead to peace.

"Moreover, they do not care if they kill females and pups!" he argued, supporting Rhudex.

Novax reminded them that they were accused of provoking the same kind of damage when they retaliated against the Selenex.

"We have the right to defend ourselves from the attacks!" spit Tradux. He proposed to end Palex's life now when they had him as close as a shot of an arrow. "As soon as we cut his head, our problem will be solved," he added.

After this affirmation, a mutinous rumbling resounded in the enormous cave that housed the palace. The inconvenience of such an act was founded in the support that many of the nations belonging to the League of Dragons gave to the Selenex. They could start a generalized war in the *Region of Fire* with such an attempt.

"The League roars much and does little," Lusux protested. "They promised us dialog with Palex to stop the attacks, and in exchange for that, many of the tribes protect them and applaud them," he accused seriously.

A similar assembly had taken place in the Selenex palace, where, as could be expected, it ended without a solution that could bring the two nations to peace.

The policies of these tribes would continue as they always had, without reason or justice. There would be no hope for its settlers.

The months went by and the war continued, with no change in the expectations of either tribe. In spite of this fact, the population miraculously reproduced beneath this climate of death, fear and insecurity.

In the middle of all this, Califax and his brothers and sisters grew up under the love and care of their mother. Novax tried to teach them the fine art of war, between games, from striking the opponent with their tail, quick movements using their wings to avoid being hit by the enemy, to fencing and military strategy. Many times the energetic youth would burn their wooden sword and shields with strapping blazes.

"Surrender abominable Selenex!" Califax threatened his brother Petrux with his sword, who in return rushed his opponent.

"Never! I would die before humiliating myself before you," he exclaimed as he breathed fire on his brother, who covered himself with his shield.

"Quiet, militant solders!" intervened Zeux, another brother. "I am a powerful Amerux who has come to impose peace, by force."

"You are no more that a frightful reptile for the gargoyles[6] to eat," said Califax, while he and Petrux rushed.

---

[6] Water-drain statues installed on the roofs of houses in the Middle Ages thought to come to life by night. (Doctors Note).

"When they learn to fly, they will be excellent warriors," Novax proudly announced to his wife, who sweetly, observed her small ones playing in the garden of the burrow.

A few months later, Califax and his brothers became members of the Royal Academy of Dragonia, an institution where only children of the Councilmen and other dignitaries of the military service could attend.

After five years of arduous study and practice, Califax, when barely had one horn on his forehead, he would have to leave home and live with fifteen other young dragons, under the supervision of Filox, exalted priest of the Royal Council, well versed with the sword and a wise dragon in the arts, history and science of his nation.

"Tell me, Califax: when was Dragonia founded?" he asked, pointing with a claw.

"It was in the year 393 of the Sacred Helion, teacher" he responded proudly.

"What nations form the *Region of Fire*, Crasux?" he asked another of his distinguished students.

"Helenex, Amerux, Anglox, Arbux, Farox, Isux, and Rhusux, teacher" he answered with a know-it-all attitude.

"Excellent! That is all for today. I will see you in a few minutes on the practice field," he said, as he rolled up the papyrus study guide.

In the stronghold where the young dragons showed their progress in the use of arms, Filox took Califax as an opponent. He spoke to the young dragon as they practiced. He told him that, Novax, his father, had also been his student, and that, years ago he had been entrusted whit an important mission which he had, unfortunately, failed.

"Do not worry yourself," he said, touching his back. "It is a very difficult mission that only very few have been entrusted with. I, myself, have failed that mission. On having finished the practice, meet me in the library and I will tell you all about it. Do not tell anybody about the mission. It is a secret."

Califax arrived that evening to the chamber of wisdom, and although he had been in that magnificent place many times, he was always impressed by the great number of papyruses that the enormous cave contained, as well as for the laurels that adorned the walls obtained by ancient heroes in many battles. Filox appeared while Califax looked around, and after greeting him, invited him to sit on a comfortable stone covered with fine mould.

"I know that you study the Papyruses regularly, nevertheless, a roll exists that you have surly not read," he said, looking for a roll in the closet, while Califax, watched with wide eyes, watching his teachers every move. "This one reveals the prophecies of Helion, knowledge of it is destined exclusively to very few dragons," he indicated unrolling the document.

"Why do only a few know about it, teacher?" asked the intrigued young dragon.

"It is best to keep these terrible prophecies from our people. They would foment great fear and confusion, making it impossible to govern the nation," explained Filox. "I will begin by reading verse three," he said, as if preparing to give a long speech: "*...And I watched the noon sky, Helion was hidden behind Selion and the Earth was surrounded by a great darkness. And then Helion sent fire and sulfur on the ungodly villages and their abominations, because he did not find anyone that spoke with justice, and later he stripped Hades,[7] of everything he had in the place where he berth, so that their souls would live forever isolated, never to see the Sacred Earth again,*" he concluded.

"What does this prophecy mean, teacher?" asked Califax, with utter fear.

"It means that our civilization will be destroyed by Helion if we continue the war against our neighbors," he clarified pacing slowly back and forth in the library.

"What do you think we can do to avoid it, teacher?" he questioned astonished.

"I will now read verse nine," he said as he unrolled the papyrus. "*And I looked at the earth and the Son of Light appeared wearing the crown of four points. Later I saw he who brandishes the fire sword come down from the sky and give the Chalice of Life to the Son of Light, and Helion drank with him, the day that his brilliance shone longer than Selion, and the nations were released.*"

"The Chalice of Life, teacher?" Califax surprisingly inquired.

"Long ago," he said, sitting next to his pupil, "a man was shipwrecked on a remote beach on our coast. One of our explorers found the man in agony, and when the man saw him, he asked: *Are you the messenger of the Highest one? Here, Sir, I give to you the secret of the Sacred*

[7] Greek God of the Hell, Identified by the Romans as Pluto. (Doctors Note).

Key so that you will become the protector and guardian of the Chalice. And, then, the man died," he said.

"A Sacred Key?" interrupted Califax who was increasingly fascinated by each word Filox uttered.

"The explorer," continued the teacher, "received a map from the man, and he, immediately, gave it to the King who ruled at that time. This map indicates three points in the region of the great islands of Briton. We have known for a very ling time that, this map, leads to the Key that will open the place where the Chalice is kept. Novalux, your great-great-grandfather was the first to try to find it, but he failed. Later, your great-grandfather, and then I went instead of your grandfather, because he became ill. Finally, your father went, but, unfortunately, he, too, failed," Filox explained, sadly.

"Why has everyone who tried, not been able to find the Key, teacher?" he inquired.

"Son, man is a very hard obstacle to overcome," he warned. "When this mission was assigned to me, I was a very young dragon, about your age, eager for knowledge and adventure. I flew towards Briton, following the map. While flying south, I saw a great dragon who was swimming in the sea, moving its wings back and forth to propel himself in the water. I flew down, to look closer, since it seemed very strange to me that a dragon should swim in that solitary expanse of water. When I was sufficiently close, I noticed that in all reality, it was not one of us, but, in fact, a ship that a group of men were navigating, with stakes whose ends were shaped something like duck's bills. The men had some type of helmet on their heads with inlaid horns on either side, and when they saw me, they raised their swords toward me while shouting *Thor! Thor!* Then, they knelt down. I sent a blaze of fire in their general direction to intimidate them and I flew away," Filox explained.

"Who is Thor, teacher?" asked Califax.

"He seems to be a god for these men who call themselves Vikings. Several of our explorers have heard them speak, and although we do not understand their language, they constantly repeat the words Viking, Thor and Odin[8], some of their other gods, I presume. They travel continuously toward the west, because it is said that they have found, a great part of the earth in that direction that we do not know about."

"Nevertheless, everyone knows that, there is nothing but the Atlantix Ocean in that direction," Califax pointed out.

"I know, son. They are just legends," he said, shrugging his shoulders. "There is nothing verified. Even so, they constantly travel to the west and they rarely disembark on our coasts, although their visits are ever more frequent. Perhaps they have discovered the land of which they speak."

"I continued flying south until reached Briton," Filox said as he rose from the chair, "and I rested near a large freshwater lake, where they say a very old dragon civilization lives, older than ours, but nobody has ever seen one of their kind. After resting for a few hours, I continued along until I arrived by nightfall, at a village that men call

---

[8] Scandinavian mythological Gods. Thor: War God. Odin: Author of Universal life. (Doctors Note).

Glas Ghu[9]. I stood on the branch of a large tree to review the map and I ignited a small flame in order to shed light on it. Even though I was careful not to be noticed by men, a small group of them surprised me. They shot arrows at me and threw rocks while shouting: *Lucifer! Lucifer!*" he vividly recounted. "Bewildered by that attack, I quickly flew away from that place.

"Who is Lucifer, teacher?" he asked, with great curiosity.

"He seems to be a malicious god that men fear," he clarified.

"How strange men are! Some prostrate themselves before you, and, yet, others attack you?"

"That is true. It is possible that some of them adore a god, while others detest that god, without considering the fact that, many times, it could be the same entity," Filox explained.

"I hid," Filox continued, "in a small cave to wait for the dawn and to continue with my day's work."

"After several days of much danger and trepidation, I reached one of the places on the map, south of Briton, close to a place called Old Sarum. There I found a strange type of construction made of enormous stones formed in a circular shape. A small group of men, dressed in strange white, red and yellow clothing, along with others who wore a red covering on their face and body. They guarded that construction that seemed to be a god's temple."

---

[9] Word of Celtic origin that means *Green Glen* (green valley) and latter became the city now known as Glasgow, in the south of Scotland, founded by Saint Ketigern also known as Saint Mungo, circa 550 A.C. (Doctors Note).

"I watched over that place for several days hoping that those men would leave for a moment, but they never did leave. It was impossible for me to approach the temple since the guards were constantly relieved. I flew towards the other two points on the map, but I found the same difficult situation in both cases: the mysterious men were there day and night and I returned to Dragonia with empty claws. The same thing happened to your father, but your great-great-grandfather and your great-grandfather, unfortunately did not have the same luck, since they never returned to the *Region of Fire*. We think the men killed them."

"Then, who will be able to find the Chalice, teacher?" asked Califax, naively.

"That is the mission that you must complete, son," Filox clarified, with a complacent smile.

"Me?" he exclaimed, embarrassed. "But, teacher, the prophecy speaks of the Son of Light," he reminded the teacher, as he rose from his chair.

"You are a Son of Light, Califax," he informed. "Your great-grandfather was born when a morning star appeared suddenly in the sky. That is why they called him Novalux, that means, *New Light*," he clarified, sitting down once again in the stone chair.

"The most recent interpretations," said Filox "brings us to the conclusion that, the four pointed crown that is mentioned in the prophecy, refers to the generations of dragons that will find the Chalice. You belong to that generation!" he said, pointing to his stunned alumni.

"Do you entrust to me this so important and dangerous mission, just because I descend from Novalux and I belong to the fourth generation?" he asked incredulously.

"No, son, that is not the only reason," he said, with his claws on his back. "Those who study in this academy are destined to occupy important positions and to do great service to the nation. You are my most advanced student, and I have chosen you for that reason. You are not obligated to take this mission, if you do not want to. Your brothers and schoolmates are also eligible members of your generation. Among them, I could find one who wants to take charge of this mission. Speak to your father, and if you decide to decline, I will understand," he clarified paternally.

"What is the greatest danger I would have to face, teacher?"

"Man, Califax," he indicated with a tremulous voice.

"Tell me about them, teacher. I do not know any."

"And you should avoid them!" he warned. "Man is unpredictable. He is afraid of his own fears. One can be of noble heart and also be a ruthless assassin at the same time. Man is worse than the most cold-blooded dragon you ever heard about," he exclaimed, with a terrified look on his face. "It is better not to risk meeting with one of them. You should be very careful, since they are all over the place. They are a pernicious plague," he emphasized.

"I will avoid them at all costs," assured Califax.

"Nonetheless, you will have to give the Chalice to one of them," Filox explained.

"Why must we give it to a man, teacher?" he asked, surprised.

"The legend tells of man who was betrayed, tortured and sacrificed, his Chalice was given to another man who collected the blood of the first man in it, where it is said that the *Light of Life* emanates. Who drinks from the Chalice will obtain the power of its glory. We believe that this legend refers to the Chalice that we are looking for. "

"Why is it necessary to give it to a man?"

"The power of the Chalice comes from a man, and a man must drink from it, first. Therefore, its power will be activated, and only in this way will it help us. After this man drinks from the Chalice, you will have to bring it back. We do not know what will happen, but once we have it, we will find out."

"Where do you think that we will be able to find this man, teacher?"

"We do not know, but we believe that the Key will lead us to him. An old astronomer from Dragonia predicted that a portion of the Earth would be surrounded by darkness, but unfortunately we do not know where it will happen, since the records where lost in an attack by the Selenex. We have never seen this phenomenon in the entire *Region of Fire*. However, we know that it will happen in approximately nine months. We have only this much time left to find the man, have him drink from the Chalice and to bring it back to Dragonia before this term expires," he explained.

"Do you think that I am the right one to carry out this mission?" asked the young dragon, doubtfully.

"If I did not believe thus, son, I would not have called you. A few more things," he added, "First: you must know that, because of the nature of this risky mission, you will be isolated. Secondly: nobody knows what I have told you, except for the King, your father and I, and it should stay that way," Filox warned emphatically.

Briton according to Filox

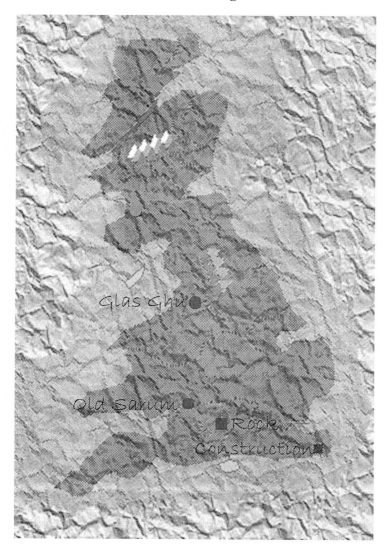

Glas Ghu●

Old Sarum■

■Rock
Construction■

Califax left the library with his head full of confusing thoughts and feelings. The ghosts of doubt that, now, distressed him terribly had never before invaded his mind. In spite of his fears, his call to destiny could not be ignored, and soon he would make a decision that would change, in one way or another, the course of the history of his nation.

However, Califax ignored the fact that there was a rumor in the Court of Dragonia, which became stronger every day, that King Rasux was keeping a secret that had only been verbally passed down, from generation to generation, by his predecessors. A secret that Filox, having promised the King, avoided reveling to his pupil. That secret would remain behind the palace walls until Califax returned, if indeed, he could return.

Anxious and worried about hiding the secret from Califax, Filox remained in the library for a few minutes more, without noticing that, while he was talking to his student, they were observed inquisitively by a sinister shadow hiding in a dark spot of the cave. Just as he had done on the way in, the mysterious shadow slipped stealthily from the library with the valuable information of the conversation that took place between Califax and Filox.

In addition to the many obstacles and dangers of the mission, Califax would have to deal with intrigues and ambushes as traitors schemed behind the palace walls.

As always, these sinister conspirators had only their own selfish interests at heart. They cared noting for the needs of the greater cause of the nation; therefore, they routinely sabotaged the legitimate aspiration of those nations who wished to live and prosper peacefully. Despite these evildoers, Califax must overcome it all in order to save Dragonia from the wrath of Helion, and from the greed of those who would interfere in the success of his mission.

The Secret of the Dragon

2

The Grand Dragon of the Chalice

C ALIFAX TOOK SEVERAL DAYS TO MEDITATE AND analyze the mission that he was offered, and he spent a few sleepless nights with the specter of uncertainty.

After listening to his fathers numerous experiences and many pieces of advice and warnings, Califax, taking stock from courage and patriotism, was named *Grand Dragon of the Order of the Sacred Chalice"*, in a secret meeting inside the enormous and cold cave of the Royal Palace.

Novax, Filox, Rhudex and other many noble dragons, who met in the enclosure for this transcendental and remarkable celebration, witnessed the solemn investiture.

In that same act, a sword with a double edge was given to him that, some time back, was given to his father Novax, who received it from the hands of a man on the legendary island of Avalon,[10] it was said to have magic powers and was made of a hard material of which the dragons not knowing.

Califax was bejeweled with a golden metal with the emblem of Dragonia inscribed on it.[11] He put it on the same chain with a reliquary locket that his mother had given him on his most recent birthday. He was also provided with a purple cape embroidered with the royal insignia.

After that he was bestowed with a red sack, which contained a papyrus copy of the map that would lead him to the Sacred Key, Califax, knelt with one knee on the ground, and then, the King, declared:

"To you, Califax, son of Novax of the ancestry of Novalux, I name you *Grand Dragon of the Order of the Sacred Chalice*," said Rasux, solemnly touching the young dragon's head with the Royal sword

The other Dragonian inhabitants assumed that Califax had been invited to travel to Amerux, to finish his studies at the academy of that nation. This belief would save his mother from unnecessary anguish, as well as the useless diffusion of Council's fears in the rest of the population of Dragonia.

---

[10] A place called Glastonbury, situated in the southwest part of England. According the legend, King Arthur went to Avalon to recover from the wounds of his last battle. (Doctors note).

[11] An eight-pointed star in a circle, flanked by dragons and two bands with a motto that said: Ad Gloriam Pater Helion (To the glory of the father Hellion). (Doctors note).

Thus, Califax, who had never left the *Region of Fire,* took flight on the dusk of that memorable day at the end of summer, on a course over the mysterious seas and to find the remote Britannic territories.

The Helenex Coat of Arms

After a few hours, Califax could barely make out the island that he called home. A feeling of melancholy pervaded. Califax controlled his fears by singing the song that he had learned some time ago at the academy.

The sea was calm and the sun fell softly on his back, and then he remembered the Viking ships that Filox had mentioned, and for that reason he decided to search the ocean far and wide, to find some of those enigmatic ships.

He arrived in the northern part of the Shetland Islands[12] and flew down to look for refuge where he could spend the night.

The wind blew softly. A beautiful full moon rose timidly as the night fell, but the strange sounds of the animals of the region, made easy prey of his tender imagination. However, he knew that he was a strong and well-educated dragon, and for that reason it would not be easy for an animal to intimidate him.

Sheltered by the soft wind of the forest, he slept through the night without another fear, and when the smooth dawn broke, he left his refuge to look for something to calm the incessant roars of his stomach.

In a nearby brook, hidden by the bushes, he found a grand variety of fish. Showing his great ability with the sword, he caught some large and succulent carps that he roasted with the fire from his nose, and then he devoured them, savoring each morsel of that delicious meat.

After his abundant and succulent breakfast, he prepared to resume his trip across the Shetland Islands to reach the Orkney isles. Perhaps it was luck, or the Law of Probability, but, just before reaching the Fair isles, he observed an impressive spectacle in the ocean. At first sight, the image seemed to arise from his imagination: seven Viking ships navigated in perfect formation filling their wakes with the cold seascape of the North Sea. With scarlet metal helmets and monumental white sails, that filled whit wind and clung to the masts as if challenge the strong gusts. They were in intense contrast against the blue ocean. The rhythmic movement of the oars, back and

---

[12] Scottish Island situated to the north of Great Brittan. (Doctors note).

fourth, quickly propelling the ships onward across the icy waters. Then, he saw the dragon's head that adorned the high-pitched sterns of the ships. Just as Filox had done, years back, Califax flew close to the ships. When the Vikings saw him, they dropped their oars, pointed their swords at him and greeted him in chorus with a thunderous cry: *Thor! Thor!* They revered the young dragon with enthusiastic acclaim.

Califax, then took out his sword, and let out a great blaze from his snout, in return for the effusive greeting. While he flew in circles over those beautiful ships, he savored the taste of what is usually reserved exclusively for the gods, after hearing, from up on high, the greeting that those faithful *subjects* offered him with such respect and admiration.

After his auspicious encounter with the Vikings, Califax had been flying for a few hours when he arrived to the southern part of the Orkney Isles. It was a place called Ronaldsay, located on the edge of the Straits of Pentland. From there he could observe, Cape Duncansby on the other side of the sea, which constitutes the northern portion of the great isles of Brittan.

However, he had suffered no misfortune, when he thought about the birthplace of his parents and grandparents, a feeling of fear and doubt nagged at him. He wondered what kind of strange beings and men could inhabit the mysterious region that he was about to enter, and what dangers awaited him. He looked around the forest for something to eat, and managed to fish in a small brook near the place where he had landed. He caught some carps with his very sharp and brilliant sword.

Night fell on the forest shawl, and the moon flirted with the thick forest of imposing Royal Pines.[13] The nighttime song of the inhabitants of that place began to manifest itself, and then Califax prepared to rest from his first emotional and exciting day.

After a while, he found a cozy place in a bend near the sea, which provided a smooth fresh bed of sweet smelling grassy herbs. He lay down in the improvised bed and slept like a log.

Califax walked inside a cold and scary cave and, when reaching the end, a gigantic man offered him a golden cup that, after drinking from it, he savored of the horrible taste of blood on his lips, and he felt an intense heat inside that burned. Then, the man guffawed: *"Would you drink of my blood, Califax?"*

The young dragon awoke in the middle of the night frightened with sweat dripping from his one and only horn. Perhaps his mind interpreted the meaning of his mission, forcing him to rationalize his horrible nightmare. "What type of man will I have to give the Chalice to?" "What will the Chalice look like?" he asked himself.

The dawn came early and Califax felt hunger pangs in his stomach. Tired of the taste of fish, he looked for something else that would provide a different taste. He missed his mother's delicious smoked turkey accom-

---

[13] The Royal pines were brought to Great Brittan and its pinecones were used as incense in many rituals. (Doctors note).

panied with roasted potatoes and blackberry sauce. She was an expert in cooking it just right, not too rare and not too well done. "Maybe, with some luck I would find some on the way," he thought, optimistically.

He crossed a part of the forest, looking mainly, for a bird, a large bird. He would even be satisfied with something with four feet to eat. Then with his sharp ears, he heard something move in the shrubs. It was an enormous and succulent hare.

Quickly, he cut the leporine off from his flight, when the hare saw the enormous jaws of the dragon; he stood petrified, for a moment with his ears up high. Califax roared ferociously and showed his sharp claws and unfolding his enormous wings. Then he rushed the unfortunate animal, whose ears seemed to melt like flowers in autumn after seeing the ferocious demonstration.

Subsequent to seeing the frightened eyes of his victim, Califax remembered that he had never killed or cooked any animal that was not a fish. He did not even know how to skin it once it was dead. Dismayed by this fact, he turned his back and let it go, only to eat some fish from the brook, again.

After a few seconds, the hare fell faint on its back, his eyes still frightened from the terror that the dragon caused her.

After eating his habitual breakfast, Califax took flight again. First, he followed along the western coast of the island in the general direction of Duncansby until reaching the Gulf of Dornoch, and once he passed there, he reached the Gulf of Moray, further to the south of

Briton, and then he flew toward the Caledonia straits, on the south west part of the island.

Since the straits become narrower until almost disappearing, he turned to the southwest, and after a few minutes, he found a great lake surrounded by beautiful mountains covered with enormous trees.[14] He stopped for a moment to admire the stunning landscape and afterwards went lakeside to drink a little water, which tasted fresh and sweet to the dragon.

Despite what you might think, dragons from Dragonia did not drink water directly with their tongues, instead they cupped their claws and brought to their snout, as any well-educated dragon would do when he has not a cup or glass.

After removing his cape, he drank eagerly from those waters when, suddenly, some bubbling caught his attention and he fixed his eyes on the phenomenon. The water from the lake was cloudy and he could not see more than a few inches from the surface. He bent closer in order to see what it was that was making the bubbles. Seconds later, a gigantic head, followed by a long neck, emerged from the water, looking like the birth of an enormous island.

The young dragon's first impulse was to flee when he saw the monster, but his sheer size hypnotized Califax, who standing on the edge of the lake.

A deep, friendly voice boomed from the enormous throat.

"Who are you, my friend?"

Califax, still astonished, stammered the answer,

"My name is Califax."

[14] Loch Ness. (Doctors note).

"Very nice to meet you, Califax. My name is Nessux," as the immense being said, making a friendly gesture with his head.

"The pleasure is mine," he said, stunned, with his claws still cupped.

"I see that you wear a Royal seal on your neck. Where do you come from? Which is your Kingdom, my friend?" he inquired.

"I am an envoy of Rasux, King of the Helenex, nation of the *Region of Fire*," he explained, rubbing his claws, nervously.

"I understand. My father told me about other members of your Kingdom who passed by this lake."

"Really?" exclaim, Califax, intrigued.

"I was barely a tadpole," said Nessux, glancing to the sky, "when my father told me that, many years ago he saw a dragon with an insignia like the one you wear. He was caught not far from here and persecuted by an angry group of men. He could not fly because of the wounds inflicted on his wings, but he made a noble stand and fought a brave battle before succumbing to the weapons of the men. Years later," he continued, "another young one like you, ran the same luck at the hands of the humans. According to what my father said, in both cases, the men called the dragon *Lucifer* while they beleaguered and attacked them without mercy."

The story from his new friend filled Califax with great pain and sadness. Surely, Nessux's father witnessed the ill-fated end of his grandparents.

"Who is this Lucifer that the men hate so much and who took the lives of my grandparents?" he inquired, with incipient tears in his eyes.

"I do not know. My father did not know either, but we believe that they confused your grandparents with that Lucifer. Be very careful, since you could have the same bad luck," he warned.

"I will," he agreed. "Men are very strange, Nessux," he said, while he played with the sand on the beach with one of his paws.

"And very dangerous!" exclaimed Nessux. "One time, a man who was fishing in the lake saw me come up to the surface for air and a little sun. A few days later, the lake was infested with them. Their intention of was to trap one of us. They came armed. Fortunately, these waters are cloudy and they could not find us.

"Us...?" he inquired with surprise.

"I am the father of a family of eight," he said proudly. "We are decedents of a very old race, the *brachiopterix*.[15] In our origins, we could fly, but once our ancestors took to the water, we lost that ability. The wings then changed to these powerful fins that now allow us to swim, even, into the deep," he explained, as he showed his large, flat extremities.

"I thought the only swimming dragons, where the Vikings," said Califax to himself.

"What brings you to this land, Califax?" he asked with curiosity.

"I am here to continue with the mission that my grandparents could not conclude."

[15] Unknown suborder of the dinosaurs. (Doctors note).

"What type of mission is it that you must risk your life for?" he asked, peculiarly.

"I must find the Sacred Chalice so that my people will not fall victim to the wrath of Helion, our god."

"Where do you think you will find the Chalice?"

"I do not know. I must first find the Sacred Key that guards it."

"It seems like an extremely difficult mission, my friend," he said rolling his eyes. "It would be better if you went on you way before the men discover you," he advised. "I wish you good luck, Califax, and if you need anything, you have friends here who will be glad to help," offered the friendly saurian.

"Thank you, Nessux. I wish you good luck too, my friend," he said, taking his leave from the gentle monster.

Califax donned his cape and took flight toward the southwest, on a course to the Gulf of Lorne. Once he was inside the Gulf, the beautiful Grampian Mountains rose on his left, where the imposing Ben Nevis Pike protrudes above the rest of the mountains at a height of 1300 meters.

The winds of the north blew softly, allowing him to enjoy the beautiful and enigmatic landscape of that golden earth, and he was glad then, that he had accepted the mission, since it presented the opportunity to see other territories and nations beyond Dragonia and the *Region of Fire.*

After flying a little more than 60 miles, he arrived at a small town called Oban, where he began to search for a refuge where he could rest and spend his other night far away from his home.

The moon illuminated the dense and dark forest of Briton, and the soft twinkle of the stars lulled the exhausted traveler, who in just a few minutes, gave in to a deep and recuperating sleep.

Califax entered cautiously into the dark and gloomy cave where the gigantic man offered him his cup. After drinking its content, the repugnant savor of blood caused an intense heat inside that burned his entrails. The horrible outbursts of laughter that emanated from the giant, sounded like a terrible omen. Then with a dangerous voice, the man asked: *"Would you drink of my blood, Califax?"*

With sweat soaking his horn, he woke up frightened, looking at the thick forest that protected him; he slumped into the melancholy company of solitude.

Hours later, timid rays of light from the sun invaded the young dragon's refuge. He awoke with a big yawn and felt tired, still. He primped the best he could, and got ready to resume his work.

Flying near Lake Fyne, he hid behind a flock of geese that glided in a *V* formation. The geese at the rear saw him, and each one of them a touched the wing of the one ahead warning them of the presence of the dragon. After warning the others of the enormous saurian, the geese fluttered desperately, increasing their speed. Then, Califax blew a smoke hoop on the tail of two geese in the rear of the formation and observed amused, the disbandment of the terrified birds, which honked insistently in fright.

After the amusement that the geese afforded him, he arrived at the delta of the Clyde River and observed the town of Glas Ghu in the distance. The Saint Mungo monastery dominated the dispersed houses made of straw, wood and large blocks of mud and stone. His anguish grew as he neared that place where men lived, and he remembered the violence with which his grandparents were treated, after they were confused with that Lucifer. He decided that he would avoid entering the town, so as not to be seen by them.

Looking for something to eat, he avoided the riverbanks, since many humans lived there. Suddenly, a mysterious sound in the forest thicket captured his attention. Curiously, he approached the tree guardedly, where those strange sounds emanated. He, timidly he looked to see a strange and uncommon animal with his back turned to him. It was chewing on something in his snout. In an untimely moment the stranger turned around, and when they saw each other, they exclaimed in unison:

"Mother was right! Gargoyles do exist!"

"Mother was right! Dragons do exist!"

Horrified, they fled in opposite directions: each trying to escape their respective childhood monsters. Nevertheless, a few meters from that encounter, they stopped.

Peeking from behind the shrubs, the gargoyle and the dragon, watched with mutual distrustful glances. Once Califax realized that he had scared that frightful being, he came out of his hiding place.

"Who are you?" he asked with a soft voice.

"Are you not going to harm me?" asked the gargoyle, with distrust, and maintaining a prudent distance.

"I will not harm you. I give you my word as a Dragon!" he assured, bringing his claw to his chest.

"Word as a Dragon...! What he does he think that means?" he asked himself. "I had only imagined them in the horrible stories that my mother told me, and now, this one is giving me his word," he mumbled with doubt.

"I assure you that I will not do you any harm, friend," insisted the dragon opening his claws and limbs, as if to show that he had no weapon.

Slowly, the gargoyle left his hiding place, keeping a safe distance, he settled on the branch of a tree.

"Tell me: What is your name?" asked the gargoyle, with a mixture of distrust and curiosity.

"My name is Califax, subject of Rasux, King of Helenex," he answered amicably.

"I do not know that kingdom. Is it very far from here?" he asked.

"It is in the *Region of Fire*, on the island located north of Briton. Tell me: What is your name?"

"My name is Hayex, I am not anybody's subject, I steal what food I can from the humans, to survive," he explained. "Indeed, you interrupted my lunch, my friend," he protested.

"I am sorry. It was not my intention, but you scared me too," insisted Califax.

"Are you really a dragon?" he asked, looking at him at great length, from top to bottom.

"Yes. Observe," he said, sending an enormous flame into the air that made the gargoyle back off.

"Are you really a gargoyle?" he doubted, looking the strange figure of Heyex.

"Of course. Perhaps look I like something else? What are you doing so far from home?" he inquired.

"I have come to look for the Sacred Key of the Chalice," announced Califax.

"A key...? What kind of key?" asked, Hayex, intrigued.

"Its confidential information," he said shaking his head 'No.'

"Where do you think it is?" he insisted in his investigative query.

"It's probably in one of these three places indicated on this map," explained the dragon, unfolding the map.

"Here there are structures made by the ancestors of the Celts, where they held ancient rituals unbeknownst to the Anglo-Saxons," he said, indicating to a place on the map.

"Why do they hide from those Anglo–Saxons?" questioned Califax, with certain fear.

"If they were to be seen, they would be severely punished. The Anglo–Saxons are trying to force the Celts to believe in Anglo–Saxons gods," he informed.

"How strange is man!" exclaimed the dragon.

"I would like very to accompany you in your search for the key, Califax," he pleaded.

"I do not know. It is a very secret mission, my friend," he said, taking his chin doubtfully into his claw.

"I know the area very well and I could help you hide from the humans," offered he excited gargoyle. "If they catch you, you will be but a mythological being, as in my mother's stories" he warned sarcastically.

"What is in it for you?" he asked.

"I have been in this place far too long and I would like to rid myself of boredom," he explained.

"Very well, but promise me that you won't do anything unless I ask you to do it," he scolded, pointing with his index finger.

"I promise!" assured the gargoyle, raising his right claw.

Califax predicted that his new companion in adventure would make a good guide in these strange lands. Judging by his looks, and his scent, it could be said that Hayex had never taken a good bath with soap and clean water. However, he hoped that his company would help him return to Dragonia very soon.

Engrossed in this new motive for enthusiasm, they did not notice that they were being watched by two sinister shadows. They were hidden in the thick of the forest as they spied and conspired.

Meanwhile, in Dragonia, Darta received, from the claws of Novax, one of the letters that Califax had written to her before he left. In spite of reading it with maternal joy, it caused her certain sadness.

"Something the matter?" Novax, sweetly, asked his wife.

"Its nothing, my love. I just worry about my little one because he is not by my side," she said, as she put the letter away.

"There is nothing to worry about, dear. I left him in good claws," he said, embracing her tenderly to calm her, and to hide his own restlessness.

"I hope so, my love."

"There is nothing to worry about," he insisted.

Meantime, the daring adventurers went towards the south, the landscape dominated by vast and beautiful plains covered with green and gilded grass. They traveled over the Gulf of Salway, until reaching the Isle of Mann,[16] where they flew near Snaefell Mountain, which has an altitude of 625 meters, and makes up the central portion of the island. They veered west and stopped close to a small town called Peel.[17]

"They say that on the island of Avalon, southwest of here, there lived a King who was wounded in battle. According to the legend, when this King was just a boy he extracted a sword that he found incrusted in a rock, in a place called Dindagel,"[18] Hayex related.

"Who can thrust a sword into a rock?" Califax, questioned incredulously.

"A man who came from distant lands did so, many centuries ago."

"And why would he do something like that?"

"They say, that a Roman soldier had thrust it into the ribs of a dying King," he related. "The man who brought it to this land plunged it into the rock so that nobody could do anymore harm with it. They say that it is a sacred relic," he explained.

"And how could the King of Avalon remove it from the rock, my friend?" inquired Califax.

---

[16] Isle of Man, in the Sea of Ireland, south of Scotland. (Doctors note).

[17] In the Celtic language, it means *Fort*. The Irish took the island following Saint Patrick's instructions, co-inhabiting the land with the Celts. (Doctors note).

[18] Now Tintagel, to the southwest of Great Britain, in Cornualles or Cornwall. (Doctors note).

"Because, this King possessed a pure and virtuous heart," he explained.

"And where is this sword?" he asked, with great curiosity.

"No one knows about it, but there is a story that says, the King of Avalon, had secretly given it to an angel before dying."

"My father gave me this sword, which a man had from Avalon gave to him. My teacher believes that it has magic powers," Califax confided.

"It looks the same as the other blades that men carry," he said with indifference, glancing at the sword.

At midday, hunger pangs made uproarious sounds in the stomachs of the two travelers. Hayex offered to go look for something especially appetizing to eat, but the dragon explained that he did not have any idea how to cook an animal. The gargoyle assured him that he would bring something already cooked by men, as only men know how to do. Califax allowed to Hayex to bring the food, since he was tired of eating carp.

"Perhaps I can bring a delicious lamb or a roasted cat," said Hayex, licking his lips.

"What kind of a thing is a cat?" the dragon asked perplexed.

"It is a feline that lives on this island. The humans call it Manx.[19] It has no tail and it is delicious," he said, licking his lips once more.

"It will be an excellent opportunity to try an exotic dish," agreed Califax.

---

[19] An anurous cat from the Isle of Man. (Doctors note).

Hayex approached one of the farms in the village followed closely by the young dragon. Wanting to be careful, the gargoyle asked Califax to wait behind the bushes, since the humans could see him very easily because of his great size. He surveyed the birdcages very carefully before committing his misdeed. After making sure that nobody was around, he flew onto the fence and began to scare the birds, provoking a great confusion in the hen house.

The great noise brought one of the farmers ran to see what was causing. Hayex took advantage of the time to silently steal into the house. Once inside, he found a delicious duck roasting over the coals, which he quickly snatched without a second thought.

With the booty in his claws, the gargoyle stuck his head out of one of the windows where he was going to make his escape, but when doing so, the farmer caught him by the neck causing his tongue stick out and his eyes to bulge from the tight grip.

"¡Papa! I found the gargoyle that fell from the roof!" yelled the man, while Hayex let the duck fall from his claws.

"Very good, son! Put it back where it belongs, at once!" he called from inside the house.

After turning and squeezing him, the farmer noticed that the gargoyle was a little bit flaccid, so he decided to fix it. He put him in a container full of wet clay so that he would harden, while Hayex fought uselessly with that clumsy and muscular man. He kicked, gagged and almost drowned, all the while screaming for help as the insipient farmer obscured his pleas behind the dim-witted words of a song.

Despite his paniced howls, Califax could not hear him: he had fallen into a deep sleep under the shade of a gigantic tree.

Once the farmer finished smothering the gargoyle with clay, he pushed him into a wood-burning oven that he used to bake bricks. After a few minutes, Hayex found himself covered with hard clay that prevented him from moving.

"It came out horrible!" the farmer exclaimed, while appraising the grotesque gargoyle figure. He went up on the roof, set the gargoyle's feet in cement, and placed him where the water drained off the roof.

The only thing that Hayex could do in that situation was to try and free his lips from the hard shell and call for his companion to help him, but he would have to wait for the farmers to sleep, in order to avoid being heard by the men.

Night fell and Hayex was still stuck to the water drainage of the house, without being able get Califax's attention in spite of his desperate cries for help. Finally, the dragon awoke from his deep sleep and he noticed that the gargoyle had not returned. "Perhaps he regretted accompanying me," he thought speculatively.

Beyond the sounds of the forest, with his highly perceptive ears, Califax could hear the moans and lamentations that seemed to come from the farm. He approached cautiously to get a better look. To his surprise, there was Hayex on top of that farmhouse, immobile as a statue, framed against the background of a full brightly shining moon, such as the one that can be seen in some theatrical and funny comedy.

After ensuring there were no humans in the area, he flapped his wings rapidly to join his companion.

"What happened to you?" he asked to Hayex, embarrassed.

"Shut up and get me out of here!" he demanded, sticking his lips out painfully from their rigid prison.

"But, how shall I do it?"

"Break the clay, idiot!" demanded the gargoyle with anger.

Califax frowned with his eyebrows after hearing that insult, removed his sword without a doubt, and struck the gargoyle on the buttocks, making him fall with a loud noise.

The noise awakened the farmers. They grabbed their weapons and ran out of the house. Califax took Hayex by the neck and quickly flew away from the place. When the farmers saw the dragon fly away, they alerted the entire village shouting "*Lucifer! Lucifer!*"

The gargoyle and the dragon went into the deep dark forest to hide from their relentless persecutors. They rested, and after they recovering their breath, Califax asked an ill-timed question of his companion.

"Did you bring something to eat?"

"What?" he exclaimed, surprised. "I almost die a horrible, terrible death of asphyxiation, and the only thing you can think of is food!" he admonished, as he shook free the remaining mud.

"You are right. Forgive me, my friend," he said apologetically.

"Forget it! It would be better if we found a place to stay the night."

They did not have to go very far to find a safe hiding spot, and after a few minutes, the adventurers fell into a deep and refreshing sleep.

Meanwhile, in the *Region of Fire*, things were getting worse. The recurrent attacks in Dragonia became more and more bloody. For this reason, the Helenex implemented operation "Defensive Wall" that consisted of patrolling, day and night, several sectors where the Selenex were known to be based. The artillery opened fire without prior indication of attack, and the armored dragons burst into the homes of those they suspected would try to secretly attack them.

In one such operation, there was a great slaughter of civilians, who, without knowing it, were used by their own military service as a shield in order to attack the enemy. The result was that the Helenex had sufficient cause to open fire on the innocent civilians: causing tremendous death and destruction. Entire families were destroyed or mutilated, causing death to some of its most important members, leaving the surviving females and pups to grieve.

The others of the governing nations hypocritically condemned the brutal attacks, and they formed a commission to investigate the regrettable acts.

These governing nations had no intention of doing a full-scale investigation because each one personally benefited from the war. They sold weapons or equipment to the warring nations. They encouraged hate among their own constituents toward allied nations of the tribes in conflict in order to acquire a more influential political position. In spite of the Helenex defense operation, the Selenex attacks caused the competence of the King to be called into question.

Rasux could not understand how the Selenex broke through the circle of defense, and at the end of several Council meetings, Rhudex insisted that they should take more harsh measures since the capabilities of the King were in doubt.

"Perhaps we should think about replacing Rasux. He is too old," he said, on several occasions without trying to hide his disparage.

Tradux reproached to Rhudex such commentary, becoming attached to the loyalty that they owed to the King. The truth is there was a traitor in the Royal Council who wanted to overthrow Rasux, while he facilitated the successful Selenex attacks.

After the unsuccessful attempt to rob food from the humans, Califax and Hayex took flight in a southerly direction after eating a breakfast of carp. They left the Isle of Man and crossed the stunning Sea of Ireland, and in a short time, they arrived to Bangor, in Wales.

As they flew over the settlement, Califax noticed much activity in the center of the village.

"What are the humans constructing, Hayex?"

"It is a temple.[20] The Celts in this region converted to the Roman gods. They are building temples of worship."

---

[20] Church dedicated to Saint Deiniol, who led the Christian Celtic community in the V century A.C. (Doctors note).

"How strange is man!" the discomfited dragon exclaimed.

They continued their passage until reaching the massif of Snowdon, where the Y Wyddfa dominated the area with its 1087-meter high peak. Below, a large number of lakes formed the valleys between the mountains, offering the travelers a beautiful panoramic view of what looked like crystalline blue mirrors.

They turned toward the east and followed the tributary of the River Dee,[21] whose falls and rapids formed abundant fluffy clouds of foam.

"They tell of a wise man, wiser than any other, who lives somewhere along this river," as he pointed to the dense forest. "His name is Dee[22] and they say that he is a powerful Magician," Hayex informed.

"Do you know him?" asked Califax.

"No. Very few have seen him, since he lives in the forest like a hermit."

"It would be very interesting to meet someone like him, my friend," said Califax.

They flew over Stour-In-Usmere[23] until reaching Old Sarum,[24] where they found a safe refuge to verify their location on the map. The map indicated three points that formed a strait line from southwest to northeast that

---

[21] Its source flows down from Snowdon and part of its tributary forms Lake Bala. (Doctors note).

[22] In this story, Hayex seems to be referring to an ancestor of John Dee; alchemist, astrologer and mathematician of the XVI century, who was the advisor to Queen Mary Tudor. (Doctors note).

[23] Now Kidderminster, southeast of Birmingham. (Doctors note).

[24] The Romans took a fort in the Iron Age that Saint Augustine called *Sarum Chant* (liturgical songs) during his trip to Canterbury. Salisbury's actual name derives from the Latin word *Sarisberia*. (Doctors note).

passed close to Old Sarum, but those points were not precise. Then Hayex remembered the ancient structures that were spread all over that area.

"Maybe, the Key is at one of these sites, my friend," speculated the gargoyle.

"But, in which one?" inquired Califax.

"We can start with Peel Dagda.[25] Perhaps we could find it there," suggested Hayex.

"What is at that place?" asked Califax.

"It is an ancient site, built by the Celtic ancestors. The Anglo-Saxons call it Stonehenge, but I prefer to call it by its ancient name," he explained.

Hours later, in Peel Dagda, from the top of a solitary tree under the protection of the night, the dragon and the gargoyle observed the Celts. There were, astonished as they watched those enigmatic men initiate a mysterious ritual, marching in a religious procession and making offerings to their mysterious gods around an enormous bonfire.

"What is it that those men are doing?" asked Califax, mumbling.

"They are preparing for the Samain," said Hayex.

"What in Helion's name is that?" asked Califax.

"It is a ritual dedicated to the transmutation of the universe. The Celts believe that all things have a spirit and that they never die, but only change form. The ritual initiates on the last day of October, when summer ends, and the ritual is extended till dawn."

---

[25]*Fort of Dagda.* Dagda was a Celtic god of the elements and storms that often represented as *Cernunnos*, god of the horned red dear. The Romans identified him with Jupiter. (Doctors note).

"How strange an animal is man!" he exclaimed.

"Not any stranger than a dragon," Hayex chided.

"Or a Gargoyle," insisted Califax.

"The Celts believe that when the sun goes down that spirits of the dead wander around the earth. The Anglos-Saxons called it Hallowed Eve,[26] and on that day some of them wander into the villages demanding a treat or they would trick them," reported Hayex.

"What kind of treat?"

"To voluntarily give every thing they owned."

"And what of the trick?" he asked curiously.

"The trick consists of destroying the village, if they refuse. After destroying the village, they place a marker in the entrance of the homes to signal to the others that the villager had already paid tribute."

"What kind of marker?" the young dragon asked intrigued.

"A candle lit inside a hollow pumpkin," he explained.

"Why didn't the villagers resist or place a pumpkin in the entrance to deceive them?" asked the dragon.

"I knew once of a deceit such as this. When, the Anglo-Saxons discovered it, unfortunately, they burned the village with its inhabitants inside," he said sadly.

"And I thought the *Region of Fire* was a dangerous place to live!" exclaimed the horrified dragon.

Suddenly, a regiment of Anglo-Saxon soldiers violently burst into the sanctuary. Califax and Hayex flew to the top of the tree to avoid being seen, and, with eyes wide whit astonishment and incredulity; they watched

---

[26]*Watch of the Sanctification.* Precursor of the present *Halloween*. (Doctors note).

the Anglo-Saxon attack the Celts. The Celts, to their credit, though they were attacked by surprise, put up a fierce resistance under the light of the full moon.

The hiss of the arrows and the cold slicing sound of metal filled the air with a funeral like wind followed by a strident choir of heart rendering howls and dying moans. People ran terrified ahead of the whinnying of the invading horses, which on many occasions trampled the men and women who lay wounded or dying.

After several minutes of anguish and desolation, the temple was assaulted by a burial silence. The inert bodies of the people ominously covered the sacred ground of the Druids.[27]

The paralyzed adventurers could not get over their horror and astonishment. They remained silent in the top of the tree without taking their eyes off that wretched scene.

After confusion took its leave, Hayex suggested to his companion that they should enter the enclosure.

"Are you crazy?" the dragon said scolding him as he clung sturdily to the tree with his claws.

"We should look for the Key, my friend," offered Hayex.

"If the soldiers return?" asked Califax.

"If they return, we will fly out. Do not be troubled; we will watch each other's backs."

They entered the place cautiously walking back to tail, avoiding stepping on the bodies of the fallen. They

---

[27] High priests of the Celts. From the Gallic, root *Dru-id* (knowledgeable in science). The Greeks confused it with the root *drus* (oak) and they applied it to the word "druids" as knowledgeable in oak (Doctors note).

inspected each stone in the construction looking to find some clue that would lead them to the location of the Key. They found only 28 cold stones arranged in a circle, many of them stained with the blood of the Celts. Within this circle, they found other rocks arranged in an elliptical form that seemed to be made to hold something in their in interior. The entire temple was surrounded by 56 strange holes in the ground, whose purpose totally escaped the imaginations of the reckless adventurers. Armed with bravery and patience, they looked for the Key with their claws in each one of those mysterious orifices, but they could not find anything, since they could not even reach the bottom of any of the holes. After long hours of searching, the dragon and the gargoyle stopped inspecting the sanctuary, and they got ready to rest from the long and exciting day's journey.

Califax felt the cold atmosphere of the cave, and it chilled him to the bone. Suddenly, a gigantic Anglo-Saxon soldier accosted him, saying: *"Would you drink of my blood, Califax?"*

He awoke in a panic roaring and shooting fireballs all over the place. He accidentally burned his faithful companion. Hayex shrieked, howled and jumped all around because the dragon had inflicted a painful burn on his tail.

"What happened...?" exclaimed the gargoyle, after putting out the fire on his tail in a nearby bog.

"I am sorry, my friend. I had a nightmare and I thought it was real," he explained ashamedly.

"I beg you to dream something else," he implored, with trepidation.

The following morning, they began to meticulously study the map. They did not know which of the points on the map represented Peel Dagda. They did not even know if any point on the map referred to the place they were currently standing. Hayex proposed that they travel southwest, to a place the Celts called Peel Lugh[28] and known by the Anglo-Saxons as Avebury, that was located 18 miles from Peel Dagda. They started on their way, and in a short time, they arrived at their destination. The view was breathtaking to the travelers.

Flanked by a pit measuring 21 meters wide, 6 meters deep and 400 meters in diameter, Peel Lugh hosted a city within its 12 hectares of land. In the center of this place there was a stone construction similar to the one in Peel Dagda, only larger. It was circled by another circle of larger rocks. From the air you could see the central trough and two central rock constructions, which constituted the ceremonial center for the village: forming three enormous concentric circles.

"How are we ever going to find the Key in such a big place?" inquired the dragon.

"I do not know, my friend. It was long ago that I visited this place and I did not remember how big it was," he answered, still astonished by the expansiveness of the site.

Despite the difficulties of penetrating Peel Lugh, the adventurers solved the problem of entering the village. In order to achieve entry, they would wait for nightfall and find a means to avoid the humans.

---

[28] In the Celtic language, *Fort of Lugh*, Druid God of the Sun, Magician and wise man. God of Gods among the Celts. Identified by the Romans as Mercury and the Egyptians as Anubis. The construction of Avebury precedes the one in Stonehenge by 500 years. (Doctors note).

While they waited for the night, it occurred to Hayex that he should find something good to eat. He stealthily approached the trough surrounding the village, which, at that time, was almost dry. He began to scrutinize the nearby farms. Then he found one that he was interested in, since the corral was filled with delicious ducks and hens, and the farmers were occupied with their tasks on the farm. He flew over the trough and the fence, and, with quick and precise movements, he snatched a pair of ducks by their necks and left the farm immediately.

Hayex flew happily back to the refuge; however, while looking back to make sure that nobody was following him, he hit a tree on the edge of the trough. The blow caused him to loose grip of the ducks and he fell into a black pit of mud. After a short time, Hayex was reunited with his scaly comrade. His body completely covered in mud, which was beginning to harden.

"I thought you did not like mud baths, my friend, but I see that I was mistaken," he said, with a mocking smile.

Hayex had to bear the sarcastic comments of the dragon, who, in order to assuage the wrath of the gargoyle, offered him various types of berries that he had gathered near the refuge.

Night fell and the inhabitants of the village prepared themselves to escape their reality through comforting dreams, and the inextricable moment to enter into the place approached for the travelers who, given their recent experiences, where overpowered by nervousness.

"I hope the soldiers do not come to this village while we are inside," Hayex voiced with concern.

"Helion forbid!" agreed the dragon, also frightened by the possibility.

Hiding behind houses and trees, they arrived to the ceremonial center of the village and, cautiously entered it. There where no doors to open, or ceilings to prevent them seeing the dark sky sparkling with stars. On the floor in the center of the construction, there were strange inscriptions all around it. Encrusted inside a huge circular rock with bas-relief there was shape that seemed to form the iris of a huge eye formed inside the structure. The adventurers concluded that this might possibly be a secret entrance to the interior of the sanctuary. They looked around the great stones surrounding the door for some kind mechanism that might open it.

After several minutes of unfruitful searching, Califax observed in the center of the rock there was a peculiarity that he had not previously noticed, due to the profound and perpetual darkness that prevailed in that mysterious and enigmatic place.

Califax lit a flame with his nose and felt around the stone, meticulously, in order to affirm his observation.

"Look, Hayex! It has a hole in the center. What do you think it is for?" he asked, looking into the disbelieving eyes of the gargoyle.

"I do not know. Perhaps it has the same function as the hollows that we found in the stones at Peel Dagda," said Hayex, scratching his head.

"Or perhaps it is an access for some kind of key," speculated the dragon.

"That is all we needed! To have to find the key for *the Key*," complained Hayex.

"Did you see this?" said Califax touching the rock.

"What is it?" questioned Hayex, as he approached the rock.

"It has strange engraved letters. What does the inscription on the rock mean?" asked the dragon.

The eye of Lugh

"It is very dark. I cannot see very well. Give me some light," said Hayex, taking Califax by the claw. "It is written in the Celtic language and it says: *Lugh will reveal its secret when a tear from the tree of the Charmer falls,*"[29] he read haltingly.

"What in Helion's name does that mean, my friend?" Califax asked with righteous indignation.

"I do not know. Let us see," reflected Hayex, taking chin in hand: "Lugh is this rock, and to the Celts, it is the god of the Sun, but I do not know what *a tear from the tree of the Charmer falls* means."

---

[29] Lug thoir an ceann dhe rud diomhor cuine coine bo-loids maighstir crann. (Doctors note).

"Then, we will have to find it out quickly, my friend," asserted the dragon.

Then, Califax's keen ears heard the sound of someone coming. Quickly they flew in the opposite direction. The obscurity of the veil of the night helped them to escape unseen.

The Secret of the Dragon

3

The Kingdom of Lugh

IN THE REFUGE CLOSE TO PEEL LUGH, CALIFAX and Hayex were discussing what the inscription on the rock meant. During the discourse, the two adventurers began to doubt each other.

"Perhaps, the key we are looking for is not here," said Hayex.

"I do not know where else we can look for it, my friend," answered the dragon.

"Remember that the map indicates a place that we have yet not visited," offered the gargoyle, pointing to the map.

"I know, but I have a feeling that it must be in Peel Lugh. This is such an important site," muttered Califax, rubbing his chin.

"The map showed a place to the southeast, where there is a huge earthen knoll," said Hayex, pointing to a place on the map.

"Are you referring to a mound in the shape of a cone, my friend?" asked Califax, scratching his head.

"Indeed," he replied. "It is a very ancient place and of great importance to the Celts. They call it Tohlmenhir[30] and they say it is the tomb of an ancient King," informed the gargoyle.

"I do not believe that it is more important than Peel Lugh," speculated the dragon.

"But, then, why is it indicated here on the map?" inquired Hayex.

"Perhaps they did it to confuse us," he considered. "The map also indicates Peel Dagda and we did not find anything there," he reminded.

"Perhaps, but we should make sure, don't you think?" suggested Hayex.

"I believe that we should concentrate on deciphering the eye of Lugh and then later, if it is necessary, we will go to the knoll," recommended the dragon.

"In that case, it will be necessary to ask for a little help," assured Hayex, scratching his chin.

"Help...? From who, Hayex?" asked, the dragon intrigued.

"Do you remember that I told you about a very wise man who lives close to the River Dee?" asked the gargoyle.

---

[30] In Gaelic, it means *High plateau of stone*, where the word *dolmen* (Monolith) is derived. A place known today as Silbury Hill. An earthen knoll, 40 meters high. The reason it was built is still unknown to this day. (Doctors note).

"We are going to ask for help from a man? Are you crazy?" he cried incredulously.

"They say it is because of his wisdom that this man is different from the rest," explained Hayex.

"After what I have seen of men, I prefer not to approach any of them," complained Califax.

"This man lives in the forest and he is not armed. Besides, we have no other alternatives to consider, unless you, yourself, can decipher the inscription," taunted Hayex.

"I hope I do not regret this," resigned the dragon.

The very idea of having to approach a man filled Califax's heart with anguish and fear. However, sooner or later, he would have to face that one of those frightful beings, since part of his mission required that he give the Chalice to one of them.

At dusk, they flew to the northwest where they crossed the Bristol Channel. They arrived at the dense place deep in the forest, somewhere close to the Snowdon Mountains and the River Dee.

Walking through the imposing weeds, the travelers hoped in some way or another, to find that mysterious wise man. The thick darkness that surrounded the forest was enough to intimidate anyone. The eerie tortuousness of the trees gave them the feeling of being in an endless labyrinth, whose walls always looked the same in any direction. The profound silence that prevailed in that strange place made the footsteps of the adventurers seem to crash on the surface of the ground.

"I do not like this place," murmured Califax.

"Me either, my friend. It is very quite and tene-brous," observed Hayex, looking all around.

Suddenly, a dense white fog engulfed them and they could no longer see each other through the fog. Cali-fax and Hayex shouted to each other in a vain attempt to locate one another, but their voices seemed to be absorbed by the fog except for strange and distorted echoes.

That strange fog disappeared as quickly as it had appeared. The dragon and the gargoyle found them-selves, without knowing it, just a few inches from one another.

They did not take even one step back when their backs touched. Both creatures were startled and they leapt wildly about screaming screams of terror.

As they stood about reproaching one another for the tremendous scare, a thin figure, covered from head to toe with a white tunic, emerged from the deep dark for-est. That figure spoke to them with gentility.

"Why have you come to this place?" he asked.

After hearing that soft, yet deep, voice, Califax and Hayex were paralyzed. Having been hypnotized by the look that came from the eyes of the ghostly figure under the hood, then Califax murmured.

"Are you the Magician they call Dee, Sir?" he asked humbly.

"Some say that I am a Magician; while others say that I am a demon," he answered, without being sur-prised before the presence of those strange visitors.

"They have said the same of me, Sir," said the dragon, pointing to himself with his claw.

"What do you want?" he asked amicably.

"I have come from a distant kingdom in search of the Sacred Chalice, Sir," explained Califax, with a courteous bow.

"And, why do you think what you seek can be found in these forests?" questioned the Magician, pointing to the thick of the wooded area.

"We have been following the indications on this map, looking for the key that leads to the Chalice," as he pointed. "We believe that it is in Peel Lugh, but we have not been able to decipher the meaning of the inscription on the stone," he explained.

"What you are looking for is only visible when it is exposed to the light," said the Magician in a somber tone.

"How can I expose to light what I'm looking for, Sir?" inquired the dragon.

"The earth soon forgets the tears of men. Only the tears of the Myrddin tree will endure in its entrails. When Caliburn returns to the rock, Lugh will divulge its secret," he said, with a strange resonance that reverberated throughout the forest.

The dense, white fog engulfed them again, and when it dissipated Califax and Hayex found themselves alone in the tenebrous forest once again.

The encounter with the Magician generated more questions than answers. However, they were single-minded about entering into the prohibited Kingdome of Lugh. They returned to Peel Lugh, where Califax reflected on the words of the Magician.

"The earth soon forgets the tears of men. Only the tears of the Myrddin tree will endure in its entrails," Califax remembered.

"The words of Dee, the Magician, are as enigmatic to me as the inscription on the stone," said, Hayex, with a hint of deception.

"Who is Myrddin?" asked Califax, curiously.

"He is a Magician who lives in the northern lands, in a forest called Broceliande.[31] They say that he has a magic tree where people go to pray or make requests. Some call him *Merlin*,"[32] he explained.

"And, why have not you mentioned this before, my friend?" he asked discomfited.

"I did not think it would be useful. When have you seen a tree cry?" asked Hayex.

"What type of tree does Merlin have, my friend?" asked Califax.

"An oak," he cavalierly answered.

Suddenly, Califax was illuminated by wisdom, and he hurried Hayex to follow him to a place he had just seen.

They flew towards a forest where oaks dominated the countryside, and then Califax began to dig at the foot of a large oak tree.

"What are you doing standing there? Help me dig!" commanded the dragon.

"But, what are we looking for?" asked Hayex.

"An oak tear," he answered.

"Are you crazy?" asked Hayex. "Oaks do not cry," he resorted.

---

[31] Close to Edinburgh, Scotland's capital. (Doctors note).
[32] Also called *The Enchanter*. (Doctors note).

"Of course they do! Help me find one," Califax ordered.

After several hours of digging holes here and there, like hard working archaeologist, Califax finally focused on a yellow object that demanded his attention in a very powerful way. On seeing the strange object, Hayex indicated:

"That is an elektron."[33]

"I think it is an oak tear," the dragon replied.

"It is an elektron. I will show you. Look," Hayex said, as he rubbed it against his body. When he brought it close to the map and the papyrus began to move towards the object.

"What a strange phenomenon. I have never seen anything like this!" exclaimed Califax with great surprise.

"The Romans used the elektron to make perfume and the Celts use it to make necklaces. I know where you can find as many as you want," Hayex informed.

"This one is sufficient. Let us go to the temple."

With the elektron in his claws, the adventurers waited for the evening to fall. Their previous experience enabled them to enter into the Peel Lugh temple with ease and confidence.

They went straight to the eye shaped rock and inserted the yellow object into the cavity. They waited, but nothing happened. Suddenly, a cloud, which had covered the moon, moved aside allowing the light of the moon to draw back the grey mantle that covered the Eye

---

[33] In Greek, it means *amber*. Fossil resin found in some plants and trees. The mathematician and Greek philosopher Tales of Mileto discovered its electrical properties in the VII century A.C. The word *electricity* is derived from the word *electron*. (Doctors note).

of Lugh. It began to shine with a powerful magnitude and intensity.

Stupefied by the unexpected brilliance, the dragon and the gargoyle observed how the great eye of stone began to move, turning its terrible stare in another direction.

When the strange process finished, the rock revealed a stony spiral staircase that lead to a secret underground tunnel.

"Do you see? It is an oak tear," declared Califax, with a satisfied smile.

They went into that long and dark passage that measured almost nine feet in height and six feet wide, and then Califax used his snout to light their way and to avoid striking his head on the ceiling. After walking only a few feet, they found several torches placed in the walls of the solid rock corridor. They lit one and continued on their journey.

It took several minutes for them to reach a junction in the corridor. It ended with a rock wall, and to the right and the left there were individual passages that curved forming a Y. After briefly deliberating which one to take, they chose the one on the right.

The brave travelers had walked for hours in the intricately connected passages of the labyrinth without finding an exit from it. While turning around in one of the recesses of that intricate place, Califax stopped suddenly causing the gargoyle to bump into dragon's tail with his head.

"Why did you stop?" asked Hayex, who was walking behind the dragon, holding to his tail, as a child takes his mother's hand to cross the street.

"After meditating long and hard," he said, finally, in a distant tone, "I have come to the sad conclusion that we have become lost and it may be impossible for us to get out of this tangled mess, my friend," Califax intoned.

"Impossible? Why do you say so?" asked the gargoyle incredulously.

"Look!" he exclaimed, as he lifted the torch to reveal a pair of skeletons lying in their path.

"What are we going to do, my friend?" Hayex whined, clinging to the dragon's tail.

"First, we must remain calm," he said with certainty. "My teacher always told me that, in all difficult situations, tranquility provides necessary character. Tranquility is the best of weapons."

"But, those men..." Hayex, trailed as he pointed his trembling claw toward the skeletons. "They had to have been in this place for weeks. Their torches probably went out and it became impossible for them to find their way in the dark. They must have died of thirst and hunger," his vivid imagination causing him to bite his claws in fear.

"Perhaps would you prefer to sit down next to these bones and wait for death?" Califax challenge as he continued along his way.

"It would be best to continue looking for the exit," suggested Hayex, looking around as if he expected to find even more skeletal remains.

After several hours of walking around that intricate place, they returned to the junction in form of a Y, and they found the passage where they had entered. Hayex suggested that they leave immediately. However,

Califax had a mission to complete and he was determined not to would not give up so easily.

"I cannot, and will not, obligate you to follow me, my friend," he said with indulgence, "but I have an important mission to fulfill for my country.

Hayex remembered that he who had insisted in accompanying Califax on this mission and it was already too late to run back. Gathering all his strength, the gargoyle continued along side the dragon.

"I would not think of abandoning you now, my friend. Let's go on!" he encouraged the dragon with certain fear in his voice.

This time, they took the corridor on the left, trying to get to the center of the circle. Within a few minutes they entered into great chamber located in the center of the labyrinth, where an enormous dome rose above them that looked like the inside of a huge Celtic soldier's helmet. It was emblazoned with engravings of carriages, suns, horses and soldiers in battle. In the walls of that vault, there were great towers of rock with niches adorned by a large quantity of horrifying and deathly pale trophies, proudly played upon their return from many bloody battles.

"What a convoluted place!" Califax exclaimed.

"These skulls must be some type of trophies," said Hayex, inspecting one of them. "The Celts cut off the heads of their enemies when captured in battle," Califax was both mesmerized and horrified at the same instance.

In the middle of that chamber, they found a great circular rock, and on the other side a passage that led to a ramp that seemed allow exit from that mortal trap. Hayex ran wildly in that direction, but he found that great stone door that blocked the exit. Tears welled in the eyes of the gargoyle.

"¡No, it is not possible...!" he cried out in panic and frustration as he repeatedly struck the obstacle to his freedom.

The Kingdom of Lugh

✛ Place of the encounter with the skeletons

● Solar Rock

Entrance

Meanwhile, Califax, keeping his characteristic calm, approached the rock in the center of the chamber. Its surface was covered with numerous Celtic emblems. He observed there was a diamond shaped hollow, in the center that was made of what looked like the top part of a lily flower engraved in the stone.

Hayex continued to wail and moan about his misfortune. He slumped against the enormous stone door and, when he lifted his head, he saw a crack with an emblem carved in it. He quickly returned to the center of the chamber to find his companion.

"What do you think is this?" asked the dragon, referring to the inscription in the rock located in the center of the chamber.

"I do not know. There is another inscription on the door blocking the exit," informed Hayex.

"I wonder what would this hollow be for, Hayex?"

"Wait! Let me see your sword," he begged. In the body of the grip of the weapon, they found a beautiful engraving similar to the one on the rock. Immediately, Califax knew what to do with the weapon. He put the tip of it into the hollow of the stone, and noticed that the blade of the sword fit perfectly into that cavity. Then, he slowly slid it in all the way to the grip, and the rapier began to shine intensely, illuminating the entire place. Right before their dazzled eyes, the stone slid to one side revealing to the astonished adventurers, a cavity that contained a small golden coffer. The sword continued to shine with great brilliance. Califax carefully removed the chest, opened it found a massive, beautifully engraved oval platter.

"This must be the Key!" exclaimed Califax, captivated by the beauty of treasure that illuminated his face.

"It is the same as the engraving on the stone door at the exit," observed Hayex.

"Remember what Dee the Magician said. *When Caliburn returns to the rock, Lugh will divulge its secret.*"

"Is Caliburn the sword's name?"[34] Asked Hayex.

"It is true. It has magic powers, just as Filox said!" affirmed Califax.

Califax removed the sword and the stone returned to its original position, leaving the chamber lit only by the torch that he carried.

Emblem of the Rock

They walked towards the exit and placed the golden plate in the hollow beneath the inscription. They watched in surprise how the enormous stone slid open to show the light of the moon in the fresh evening air. Once it opened all the way, Califax removed the plate and put it in his

---

[34] Ancestral name for Excalibur that, according to Thomas Malory, which means sharp steel. (Doctors note).

bag leaving the place cautiously, before the stone returned to its resting place to seal the enclosure perfectly.

Once outside, they noticed that they were on the slope of a hill. Hayex flew to the top. He was embarrassed to find that the mound that they were on was in fact the Tohlmenhir mound.[35] The winding underground passageway connected the sanctuary and the mound. The gargoyle and the dragon, miraculously, had found the way out from the winding pathway kingdom of Lugh.

After that adventure, the tired companions flew to their refuge in the forest to sleep, for rest of the night, the sleep of the innocent.

Very early, in the morning, before Hayex woke up from his deep sleep, Califax went about the task of analyzing the Key. It was an oval object made of pure gold similar to a medallion, with many engraved symbols. On the top of it, there was a star similar to the Helenex coat of arms, but with twelve points. Under the star, there was an elongated inverted triangle that pointed at what seemed to be a base in form of a half moon. The triangle and the half moon formed, altogether, a cup from which a star emanated. On either side of the cup, there were indecipherable symbols for the dragon's eyes.

Hayex woke up heavily from his sleep, and after a brief morning greeting, he noticed a strange inscription on the back of the medallion as Califax, captivated, scrutinized the front of the treasure. This inscription said $IX\Theta Y\Sigma$ [36] in big letters.

---

[35] Silbury Hill (Doctors note).
[36] Greek word pronounced as *ICHTHUS*. (Doctors note).

"What do you think it means, Califax?" asked Hayex, intrigued.

"I do not know, my friend, but we have not become expert interpreters. We will have to ask for help, again, my friend."

As if reading each other's minds, the gargoyle and the dragon got ready to ask Dee the Magician for help. They did not know that they were being watched from the darkness of the forest by two sinister figures: two evil dragons who conspired against them.

"Lets take the Key now, while it is within our reach," said one of the conspirators.

"¡No! Our orders are to relieve them of the Chalice once they obtain it," reprimanded the other.

"Perhaps they will never find it."

"If they fails trying, then we will take the Key. Only until then," he declared.

Califax and Hayex flew to the place where they had found Dee the Magician, and they went into that dismal place in the forest. Once again, the thick fog covered them with its mysterious mantle and seconds later, the Magician appeared.

"What is it that you want?" the magician asked, kindly.

"We have found the Key of the Sacred Chalice, Sir, but we do not know where we should take it," explained Califax bowing before him.

"The fish is the fisherman and his dwelling the east sea, from where the cross came to join with the sun."

Dee said nothing more, and just as the fog appeared, it thus dissipated. As before, the adventurers were left with more questions than answers. However, Califax was confident that he could decipher the mysterious lexis of the Magician. He knew the answers where in his words.

"I think that Dee has gone crazy. How is it possible for the fish to be the fisherman?" inquired Hayex

"...*From where the cross came to join with the sun,*" he remembered. "Which cross is he referring to?" asked Califax.

"Some Celts converted to the Roman gods they held services using a cross inside of a circle.[37] Perhaps it is the cross that Magician is referring to," speculated the gargoyle.

"It is possible that the circle represents the sun, but, wherefrom did the cross come and what does it represent?"

"I do not know. The Romans brought it a long time ago. The Magician mentioned an eastern ocean. Perhaps it comes from there," offered Hayex.

"When we were flying over Bangor," he remembered, "I asked you about an edifice that the humans were building. It seems to me that I remember seeing a cross."

"That is true! It is a temple erected for the Roman God," he agreed.

"Perhaps we can find out more about this cross in Bangor, don't you think?" reflected Califax.

---

[37] Celtic cross or *Triskel*, whose symbol is, ☧. It represents the trinity of Gods formed by Tutatis, Esus and Taranis. For the Christians, it means the predominance of the faith in Jesus Christ over the adoration of the sun. (Doctors note).

After flying a few hours on a northwesterly course, they arrived at the town of Bangor. The church of Saint Deiniol was being built on a large piece of land, and it surrounded by a great stonewall.

The Key of the Sacred Chalice

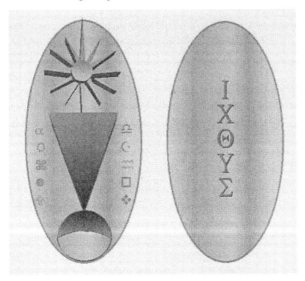

A few meters from the temple a great bell tower rose. It resembled a great silo with large windows at the top of its slender body, and finished with a reddish conical roof, as a rocket that indicated the place of its destiny. The houses of the clergymen were made of white blocks that resembled igloos. The white blockhouses completed this complex dedicated to Christian faith. As usual, Califax and

Hayex would have to wait for the cover of night to evening to furtively enter into the hermitage.

Protected by the blackness of night, the daring adventurers entered the church by means of an open window. Once inside, the vaulted ceiling amplified the sounds that they made as they tried in vain to be quiet. The dragon lit a fire with his nose, and when they got to the pulpit they found a great cross leaning on the main wall.

"Who is that man on the cross?" asked Califax.

"*INRI*," said Hayex, after seeing the sign placed atop the cross.

"It is a very strange name, don't you think, my friend?" indicated Califax.

"Why did they crucify him?" asked the intrigued gargoyle.

"I thought you would know, my friend," said Califax, turning to look at the gargoyle.

"Wait a moment. There are several words below the name," he said, drew nearer the cross. "*Iesus Nazarenus Rex Iudaeorum*," read Hayex, with difficulty.

"Then, *INRI*, is not his real name, my friend. It is Jesus," corrected Califax.

"How do you know it? Do you know this language, Califax?"

"Of course! Latinux classes are obligatory in Dragonia."

"What does the inscription mean?"

"It says: *Jesus of Nazareth, King of the Jews.*"

"Why would the humans have crucified a King?" Hayex asked, surprised.

"How strange is man!" seconded Califax with astonishment.

"Perhaps, Nazareth is the place where the cross comes from," observed the gargoyle.

"Maybe, but, where is that place located and who are the Jews?" inquired Califax.

"Listen, my friend, Why do you think I should know everything?" he asked annoyed.

"I was only asking," clarified the dragon.

"Perhaps we can find a map here that indicates the location of that place," indicated Hayex

"Silence!" he interrupted alarmed. "Someone is coming," alerted Califax. They quickly flew to a wooden beam that supported the roof of the church.

The door opened slowly, and a very plainly dressed man entered the church, illuminating his way with an oil lamp. He looked around the place and went through the side door to a place where the dragon and the gargoyle had not noticed.

The great weight of the reckless intruders burdened the crossbeam, causing it to squeak and sag slightly. However, they remained motionless as they silently prayed that the wood would resist until the watchman left.

After making sure that everything was in order, the man left the place in a leisurely fashion. They came down from the beam and went directly to the secret door. They hoped it would information to help them find their way to the Chalice. They reached the door only to find it locked and strongly fortified. A long time passed while they tried to discover a way to open that mysterious room, but time and time again, they heard the categorical refusal of the lock to let them in. Then Califax took his sword out and introduced the tip of it into that obstinate door lock. The sword began to shine intensely, as it had in the labyrinth of Lugh. Slowly he turned the rapier and the door, magically, opened. They entered a room that seemed to be the sacristy of the church, and Califax stuck his head in to light the room with a flame from his nose. The place was filled with papyruses. They hoped that one of them would contain the information that they were looking for.

"Where did this large amount of papyruses come from?" asked Hayex.

"Since they are written in Latinux, perhaps the Romans brought them," observed Califax, while he looked at the large number of documents.

"It must be, because the Celts did not write.[38] The Bards[39] sang their history," informed Hayex.

"Look, Hayex! I found a map of the Roman Empire," he exclaimed as he unfolded the map on the table.

"The Romans are great conquerors. Look at the size of their empire!" Hayex indicated, astonished.

"Here, to the east on the map, there is a province called *Iuda*,"[40] observed the dragon. "The plaque on the cross says that the man was the King of the Jews, which in Latinux is *iudaeorum*. This must be the place the cross comes from," he asserted.

---

[38] Along with the evangelization of the Celtic people, the monks, introduced the Latin alphabet, little by little, that gave origin to the first Celtic written language, called Gaelic. (Doctors note).

[39] Celtic jester that orally transmitted the history and accomplishment of the Celts. (Doctors note).

[40] Judah or Judea. Palestine region of present day Israel. (Doctors note).

"Are you sure?"

"Remember that Dee the Magician mentioned an ocean to the east, and this map also shows an ocean called Galilee."

Suddenly, Califax heard the door to the temple open. The adventurers were trapped inside the room; they would have to devise a way to get out without being seen. There was only one exit: the door. The light of the lamp became more and more intense, while the man condemningly walked directly toward to the room where they were standing. They would never be able to escape from that door.

"Who is there?" with a tremulous voice, asked the man from the threshold.

The watchman did not obtain an answer. He saw the door halfway open. He cautiously opened it wide and held it open with a trembling hand, with the lamp high over his head. He stopped at the jamb of the entrance, and moving the lamp from one side of the room to the other, he examined the entire location, but he did not find anything.

Up on the ceiling, Califax and Hayex clung to one of the beams in the library, precariously holding the large number of documents that they had borrowed from the shelves. The documents were in danger of slipping from their claws at any moment.

The time that the man remained into the room seemed eternal for the explorers, who began to fall victim to nervousness. The wooden beam seemed to accuse the invaders with its constant spiteful squeaking, but the distrustful monk did not notice. To make things worse,

Hayex, also held a map in his snout, and watched with anguish how a drop of sweat crossed his nose, causing a slight tickle that threatened to turn into a sneeze and expose their intrusion. Califax saw that his friend was on the verge of violently expelling the document and he quickly placed his tail under the nostrils of Hayex and avoiding the sneeze.

"How strange! I am sure that I locked this door with the key," he said looking all around. "Perhaps, the light that I saw from my room was a reflection of a falling star," the man explained to himself.

The man was sure had forgotten to close the door last time. He locked the door with the key, and returned to bed.

After that tremendous scare, the adventurers hurried down from their improvised hiding place. Califax packed the map of the Roman Empire before leaving the temple of Saint Deiniol.

Despite being locked up, they repeated the formula that they had used to enter the library: Califax removed the brilliant sword and introduced it into the lock again and, magically, the door opened again.

Once in the hermitage, they hurried to reach the window from which they had entered. Just a few meters of freedom, they could make out the figure of the watchman who returned hastily to the enclosure.

When the watchman saw the dragon and his repulsive companion he screamed, *"Lucifer! Lucifer!"* He alerted, in a very loud voice, the rest of the acolytes.

The adventurers hurriedly took flight. They could hear the shouts of the listened to the outcry of the inflamed clergymen as they cursed the presence of those *'diabolic'* intruders who had dared to profane the sacred ground of the church of Saint Deiniol.

Church of Saint Deiniol

This moment would mark the beginning of great and exciting adventures, where they would confront the mysterious and distant territories of the Middle East.

The Secret of the Dragon

4

The Oracle of Apollo

THE DRAGON AND THE GARGOYLE LEFT THE TOWN OF Bangor taking a course to the southeast. During the voyage, they were hit by a sudden and persistent storm that made their journey slow and hard. Additionally, uproarious wind and blinding lightning threatened to knock the wet travelers out of the sky.

Extremely tired, Hayex could no longer manage to maintain the strong pace of Califax, who with a renewed spirit, flapped his wings as if he to challenge the force of Mother Nature. Taking hold of his companions tail, the gargoyle allowed Califax to drag him sluggishly using the dragon's vast powerful wings that he flapped in time like a powerful motor.

After a few hours, they arrived at a place where the wind and the rain took pity on the travelers and gave way to the reddish sun of the dawn.

"What city is that?" asked Califax, with great curiosity.

"Its name is Londinium,"[41] informed the gargoyle. "The Romans founded it on the banks of the river the Anglo-Saxons call Thames. It is the largest city in the Kingdom of Essex. The river is used to transport soldiers and merchandise from the ocean to the entire region," he indicated with a know-it-all air.

"Do you know what that enormous circular construction is, Hayex?" asked Califax, pointing to edification with a claw.

"It is an arena. My grandfather told me once that slaves, men and women, fought to the death to amuse the Romans. They called them *Gladiators*. Many times, they fought against ferocious beasts brought from distant lands."

"What? As if they don't have enough death with the wars they rage among themselves? How strange is man, my friend!" he exclaimed perplexed.

Following the channel of the River Thames, they left the populated city of Londinium behind. They took toward to the city of Canterbury, that it is located in the southeastern end of the Island of Briton.

They circumvented the city trying to avoid being seen by men, before venturing out to the Straits of Dover.

---

[41] Ancient name of the city of London, founded by the Romans in the year one B.C. (Doctors note).

"Here lived a man who predicted that, this city would be destroyed by the Roman fire god," informed the gargoyle.[42]

"It seems that the preferred weapon of the gods is fire," observed Califax.

"Not only of the gods, my friend," he said. "My grandfather told me that, in very remote lands, men discovered a way to send fire greater distances. Just imagine the wars that could be raged, once the invention becomes well known!"[43]

"Many times, reality surpasses the imagination. I imagined what the wars could be like in Dragonia, but I never thought they could be so bloody till I saw one with my own eyes," clarified, Califax.

"That is true. Before meeting you, I could only imagine how ugly dragons could be," said Hayex, with sarcasm.

Continuing along their route, the dragon and the gargoyle crossed the Straits of Dover pass until reaching the beautiful coast of Calais, in Gallia Comata[44] that, at the time, was dominated by General Clotaire II who governed the ferocious Francs.

Since the victory of Merovech over Attila the Hun, in the Catalonian fields in 451, the Francs already governed four Gaul regions: Austrasia, Neustria, Aquitania

---

[42] According to legend, in 619 A.D. Saint Mellitus saved Canterbury from the divine fire thanks to his prayers. (Doctors note).

[43] Hayex is probably referring to the use of gunpowder in fireworks, in China, between 605 and 614 A.D. (Doctors note).

[44] *Gaul of the long hair.* The name given by the Romans to the Celts that mixed with the original inhabitants in the territory located between the Pyrenees, the Alps, the Rhine and the Atlantic Ocean, giving rise to a new people: the Gaels. (Doctors note).

and Burgundy, which Clovis the First later divided among his successors.

In these lands, disputed by several Barbarian peoples,[45] the valiant explorers initiated a new and exciting stage of their adventure.

In an area near the fishing village of Calais, they stopped to take a rest and decide what to eat before continuing with their journey. The fish diet was not in their plans, for which Hayex, decided to entertain Califax with a succulent suckling pig that he himself would stew for the dragon.

From the top of a huge tree, the gargoyle watching carefully before he approached to a small farm and descried a litter of piggies whose mother was away from her young. Hayex took the opportunity to take one of those delicious creatures. Gliding quickly, Hayex rushed one of the pigs to catch it in-flight, but the great weight of the piggy prevented good maneuverability.

Despite his inability to take the pig in-flight, Hayex grabbed the squealing piglet and walked briskly toward the forest on the other side of the farm. He tried in vain to silence the pitiful squealing of the pig. When he turned the corner of the property, the would-be thief came face-to-face with the furious, indignant mother. Hayex, with a sheepish smile, slowly and gently put his booty on the ground and patted the head of the young pig. The mother attacked the gargoyle with a burly butt of her head sending him headlong into the pigsty. He landed as a rocket on a target, leapt to his feet and fled

---

[45] At the fall of the Roman Empire, the Barbarian people burst violently into Gaul: Francs, Goths, Suevis, Saxons, and Germanic tribes. (Doctors note).

covered, again, with mud. He was hurrying to get away and to get the mud off before the sludge hardened and turned him into a grotesque statue again.

Hayex was very upset when he met up with his hungry companion.

"Thank heavens that this time, they did not cook you in a furnace and place you on a roof, my friend," said Califax making fun with outbursts of laughter at his comrade's propensity for misfortune.

"I can just see your face when you are eating a *delicious* roasted carp," he threatened, while he cleaned the mud off his body.

After reluctantly eating some fish, the adventurers got ready to take an invigorating nap. The evening in Bangor had been very exciting and the trip through the storm had taken its toll on the traveler's strength, for which they decided to dose a little.

Califax found himself trapped in a cold and humid cavern, while he listened to the uproarious echo of his own steps. Suddenly, the shadow of a gigantic man raising his cup, projected on the wall in front of the dragon. *"Would you drink of my blood, Califax?"* he asked with a deafening outburst of laughter.

He was startled awake and he started sending flames left and right. One of the flames hit the tail of his companion again. Hayex yelped and howled as he jumped around in the weeds until he reached the brook to extinguish the fire on his blackened backside.

Map of Briton

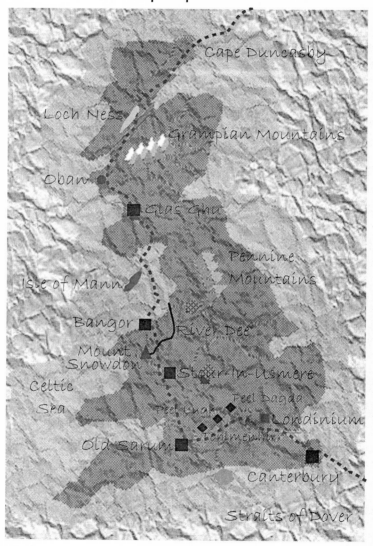

After that embarrassing incident, the intrepid adventurers resumed their journey. They traveled toward the southeast to cross the difficult and uneven mountain range of the Alps.

As they flew over the vast river basin of Paris, they crossed the green prairies of the province of Champagne. Finally, they reached the plateau of Langres, in Burgundy, leaving behind them the city of Dijon and the valley of Saône. Before them, the extensive walls of the lower Alps hid a valuable treasure, the spectacular Lake Leman.[46] They stopped to take a drink of its cold pure waters. The view from the lake was no less spectacular than the one that was offered from the air, and the anxious travelers could not stop marveling before the immense beauty of the vast countryside.

"The world is a splendid place to live, don't you think, Califax?" said the gargoyle, ecstatically looking all around him.

"But of course, my friend," he agreed nodding his head. "I hope future generations take the time to appreciate it and preserve it."

Suddenly, the sky was filled with a strange sound followed by violent tremor, taking the thirsty travelers attention away from the beautiful lake. A gigantic Burgundies[47] army of soldiers on the southern slope of the mountain was sent to lead an attack on the followers of the Francs in the valley commanded by intrepid and val-

---

[46] Named by the Swiss as *Lake Geneva*. (Doctors note).

[47] Scandinavian people from the island of Bornholm, in the Baltic Sea, they invaded Galicia in 406 B.C. They helped the Romans in the V century, establishing a powerful Kingdom near Lake Geneva. (Doctors note).

orous Chlothar.[48] From their refuge in the forest, the dragon and the gargoyle observed the battle that was staged in that esplanade.

The Burgundies rushed the Francs in a violent swell. The Francs stood like statues in the formation of a square under the precarious security of their shields. A few yards away, the Francs soldiers threw several gigantic ropes in front of the Burgundies, and raised enormous traps in the form of scissors made out of pointed wooden stakes. Those enormous hooks horribly goaded a large number of men and beasts.

Once the mortal barricade was drawn, there was an intense hiss of lances and arrows. The horrible sound of swords striking heads, along with the whinnies of the noble horses, made up an ominous choir to accompany the suffering moans of the dying and wounded. The earth, before an immaculate green and ocher color, was now intermingled with the blood and carnage of men and horses, turning the landscape into a chaotic and grotesque surrealistic scene. The cruelty of the soldiers in the battle stupefied the horrified witnesses at the carnage even more.

After a few horrifying and bloody hours, the battle finally languished. The disciplined Chlothar forces had overcome the Burgundies. They fled in a mad dash toward the mountains, where they would regroup to look for revenge for the defeat inflicted upon them.

They had fallen behind in their schedule while watching that horrible spectacle. They hurried to fly across

---

[48] King of Neustria that took control of Austrasia and Burgundy, in 613 A.D. In the following year, he founded the capital of the empire in Paris. (Doctors note).

the Alpine Mountains. The horrified travelers maintained a long silence between them, like the silence at a funeral.

When they arrived at Mont Blanc whose peak rises above the other mountains and snowy coat, the travelers seemed very small indeed before its 4800 meters in altitude. However, they felt more alive and privileged than ever to be able to view the magnificent work of the Creator.

The surprises would augment with the distance. When they crossed the boarder of Italy, in the Piedmont Alps, and over the Gran Paradiso Mountain reigning at 4060 meters. The Etruscan rural provinces welcomed them. The beauty of the countryside seemed to evoke the beautiful words of the illustrious poet Virgil: "All hail, O earth! All hail, my household gods! Behold the destin'd place of your abodes!"[49]

Following the indications on the map, they traveled over the plains and over the Po River, in the dominion of the once unbeatable Roman Empire. Flying over the coasts of the Tirreno Sea, throughout the Liguria and Toscana regions, they reached Mount Amiata and flew over Lake Bolsena. Once in the Straits, they decided to make a short stop at Lake Bracciano.

"Have you noticed that this lake is at a very high altitude?" observed Hayex.

"Of course! The Lake is formed inside the crater of the volcano below us. You can taste a slight taste of sulfur in its waters," he explained offering a drink.

"It tastes horrible!" exclaimed the gargoyle, after taking a drink.

---

[49] The Aeneid of Virgil, Book VII. (Doctors note).

"Drink a little more. Sulfur is good for your health in suitable amounts," said Califax.

"It maybe good for the health of a dragon."

The adventurers flew towards the southeast, on a course to the River Tiber. They stopped in a wooded place, to the south of Rome, close to the Portuensis road. Califax unfolded the map and determined that they were in the suburbs of the legendary capital of the powerful Roman Empire.

"Did you know, my friend, that Rome was set on fire by its King?" asked Hayex.

"What did you say?" he exclaimed incredulously.

"It is true! My grandfather told me that King Nero set the city afire, and blamed the first people to adore the Roman god."

"How strange is man! While I have to complete the mission that will prevent Helion from setting Dragonia on fire, men take it into their hands to set their own cities on fire."

They followed a course along the boot of the Italian coast. As they flew, they surveyed the beautiful earth below. On their left, they saw a great bulge that formed the Penino Alps drawn in the distance, and on their right, the blue Tirreno Sea. When they arrived at Calabria, they laid course to the Ionian Sea, where Mount Pecoraro dismissed them with a cold good bye, from the heroic land of the legendary Aeneas.[50]

The sea was calm and the travelers seemed to have floated into that blue immensity. They flew slowly

---

[50] Latin hero of the Trojan War, cousin of Hector and Paris, immortalized by "*The Aeneid*" of Virgil. (Doctors note).

and smoothly, as the Roman galleys had done, but their thoughts were as agitated as the frenetic rowing of a galley slave, chained forever inside the ship gloomy entrails.

After several minutes of tacit traveling, the adventurers arrived at the Ionian Islands. They passed by the straits formed by the Levkas and Kefallenia islands to finally arrive at Ithaka, that awaited them as Penelope waited the arrival of Ulysses after his long odyssey.[51] The travelers flew down to the mythical island, where they looked for a refuge and something to eat. The dragon decided to continue with his diet of fish, after the gargoyle offered a pair of delicious rats that were at least to the fine palate of the dragon, a delicacy more than repugnant.

The afternoon sun covered that beautiful island with its reddish mantle just outside the Gulf of Corinth, and they decided to rest there for remained of the day. They unfolded the map to find their position and prepare for their trip the following day.

"The most accessible area to cross Greece is through the Gulf of Korinthiakos," indicated Califax.

"One time, I heard my grandfather say that, here, very close to Mount Parnassus, there is a temple called Delphos,[52] where a priestess predicts your future."

"You do not believe in those things, right?" asked Califax.

"They say she is very accurate in her predictions," replied Hayex.

---

[51] According to Homer, Ulysses (Odysseus) reigned on the Island of Ithaka (Ithaki) when he left to war against Troy. After ten years of nomadic sailing, he was reunited again with his wife Penelope. (Doctors note).

[52] Delphi. Located on a slope of Mount Parnassus, 10 kilometers from the Gulf of Corinth, between continental Greece and the Peloponnesus. (Doctors note).

"Even if that were true, how could we consult with her? If the humans see us, I could not augur very good things."

"The place is on the way. Once there, we could find a way to consult with her. Perhaps she will give us some information about the Chalice," insisted Hayex

The light of dawn hardly illuminated the incipient day, when the adventures resumed their trip. They flew towards Corinth, as they had planed, and in a short time, they arrived at the imposing Mount Parnassus. While looking for the Oracle of Delphi, they found an enormous site in ruins. Rocks and columns lying here and there indicated that a catastrophe had recently affected the place that created the current chaos. Apparently, it was deserted, and for that reason they decided to land to investigate. They flew down in the middle of a large collection of stairs that where arranged in such a way that the half moon that cut down the middle faced toward an esplanade.[53] The footsteps of the explorers resonated in the enclosure with an open area skyward. They walked further and came up a conical stone,[54] similar to a Celtic soldier's helmet, which they admired in silence for a while. Latter, they walked up a ramp that seemed to lead, in another time, to the main entrance to the temple.

A penetrating smell seized the atmosphere, and Hayex then, remembered the taste of the waters at Lake Bracciano in Italy, it was similar to the smell at the Lake.

---

[53] The Dionysus Theatre. (Doctors note).
[54] The Navel of the World. The place where two eagles meted sent by Zeus from the extremes of the world. (Doctors note).

"It seems this place is empty," whispered Hayex, sticking his head into the threshold of the enclosure.

"Let us enter. Perhaps we can find something interesting," suggested the dragon.

Rocks and effigies littered the floor of the temple; Califax and Hayex went into an underground room illuminating their way with a flame the dragon had lit with his nose. After reaching the end of the adytum,[55] a murmur arose in the lugubrious room illuminated by a great flame.[56]

"Come in, tired pilgrims, eager for wisdom and knowledge," an old feminine voice encouraged them to come closer to the Kassotis spring.[57]

The adventurers stood petrified feeling exposed in front of that strange woman with snow-white hair and a face grieved by the profuse wrinkles plowed by Cronos.[58] Nevertheless, once they got a closer look, they could see that she was blind.

Once they were sure of that fortunate fact, the pressure in their chests was relived.

After observing the place for a few moments, the adventurers dared speak to the woman.

"What place is this?" the dragon asked, very intrigued.

---

[55] Subterranean area where a pythoness made predictions. (Doctors note).

[56] The Eternal Flame. (Doctors note).

[57] Name of the part of the aqueduct that transported water to the village of Kastri, constructed by the Romans around 385 B.C. The pythoness bathed in its waters before prophesizing. (Doctors note).

[58] Uranus, Cronos' father, announced that one of his children (Zeus) would overthrow his rule. To protect his Kingdom Cronos devoured all the children he engendered, just as time does with us. (Doctors note).

"This temple is the dwelling of Apollo," she answered cautiously. The woman was sitting on a tripod while she held laurel leaves and a beautiful copper vase.

"But... What happened? Why is it all in ruins?" asked Califax, disturbed.

"I am Pythia, the last pythoness. Theodosius sent Typhoon to engulf this sanctuary in great flames.[59] Years later, it was reconstructed, but Gaia, jealous of Apollo, shook violently to destroy it,"[60] she said.

"Who is Typhoon?" inquired, Hayex.

"The dragon with one hundred heads conquered by Zeus. It lives in the entrails of Monte Etna, and its moans can be heard in this temple," she explained, pointing out the sulfur emanations that Hayex had noted before.

Califax waned before that horrible story. Gazing all around him, he looked for Zeus, as if to prepare to save his scales from the wrath of the terrible Greek god. After a few seconds of ceremonious silence, the pythoness asked,

"Tell me your names and what you want to know."

"My name is Califax and I come from very distant lands. I have come looking for the Sacred Chalice and I desire knowledge of where I can find it."

Then, deeply inhaling the heavy air that emanated underneath the tripod, the priestess extended her hands

[59] Before dividing the Empire between his children Arcadius and Honorius, Theodosius the First ordered the temple to be set on fire along with other pagan temples in 385 A.D., with the purpose of imposing Christianity. (Doctors note).

[60] In the beginning, Delphi was devoted to Gaia, Goddess of the Earth. An earthquake destroyed the sanctuary in 548 B.C. (Doctors note).

to the top of the temple, and with a haunting voice, she said,

"The fish is the fisherman who throws his nets in the desert."

After hearing those words, the daring adventurers glanced at one another strangely. Califax then asked,

"Will the Chalice save my country?" inquiring with certain hope.

"Whom that is hiding in the dark, inquires: *Would you drink of my blood, Califax?*" she answered ecstatically

After those fateful words, the dragon and the gargoyle ran quickly away, falling and tumbling among the rocks and statues on the temple's floor. The frightful, recurring nightmare of Califax seemed to have come to life in the words of that mysterious clairvoyant.

A handful of men and women that were walking to the temple, watched overawed by the sight of the flight of the *'diabolic figures'*. After recovering from their surprise, the villagers assigned an unjust epithet to the two frightened travelers: "*Typhoon! Typhoon!*"

The dragon and the gargoyle flew at full speed and in a panic. They were almost out of breath, and Califax seemed to be navigating without a course. After a few minutes of intense confusion, Hayex calmed his scaly guide. In a wooded place not far from Delphos, they rested to recover and let the original color of their faces return.

Still scared by the words of the pythoness, Califax asked if the adventure that he had undertaken was destined to failure or if it would lead to the unlucky end of his life. When Hayex saw the dragon's confusion, he tried to convince him to continue with the mission.

"You cannot give up, now! I assure you that we will find the Chalice, soon," he assured Califax.

It did not take long to rescue Califax's enthusiasm for continuing with the adventure of their mission. After all, Filox and the King, from among many other candidates had chosen him. He could not fail. The hope of the Court of Dragonia had been set on his back, and he had already reached the point of no return. He decided to continue until the end, and confront the future with the same strength of character and commitment that his ancestors had shown in the past.

They took a course towards the city of Athens, where they would investigate the enigmatic words that the Oracle at Delphi, and Dee, the Magician, had uttered.

"We should find out what *the fish is the fisherman* means," asserted Califax.

"Not only that, but what the inscriptions on the medallion mean," reminded Hayex.

In the woods near the Athenian market, Hayex devised a plan to complete his investigative objective. First, he would pillage a cape from a villager who, languished in the arms of Morpheus at the foot of a great tree. Once he had the cape in his possession, he would place it on his back and over his head in order to disguise himself. After this, he would go to the town and inquire about what the inscriptions on the medallion means to some merchant.

Hayex stealthily approached the innocent man to snatch his cape. However, the man embraced his cape as if it where his beautiful *fiancée,* and it would take somewhat more than a simple tug on the cape to take it from the man. Hayex was inspired. He asked Califax to blow a few small flames close to the tree where the man slept, but to be careful neither not to burn him nor to wake him. The ruse worked perfectly. After a few warm blazes, the man drew back the thick cape that covered him. Hayex did not waste any time taking the booty, and both of them fled after committing the holdup.

Califax could not repress his laughter upon seeing the humorous figure of Hayex dressed in the cape. Hayex was only 37 inches in stature: he could scarcely pass as a *"warmly dressed gnome"* according to the sarcastic words of the dragon that he professed while trying to drown the weeping that the outbursts of laughter had caused him.

"Very funny!" he said very seriously with his hands on his hips. "I will pass myself off as a boy!"

"Tell me, my friend," he said, speaking with difficulty, "How do you think you are going to hide those frightful feet from the eyes of the men?" between sonorous outbursts of laughter, while he pointed out the claws on Hayex's feet that could be seen under the cape.

"Stop laughing!" Demanded the gargoyle furiously. "You will take the shoes off the man so I can wear them!" he ordered, pointing at him with the index portion of his claw.

"What?" Califax exclaimed cutting abruptly his shorts outbursts of laughter.

The adventurers returned to the place where the man still dozed peacefully. With extreme caution, the dragon approached from behind the tree to warm up his feet, and after repeating the operation two or three times, the villager began feel discomfort of the heat on his feet.

After a short while, the man chose to take off his shoes, all the while keeping his eyes closed so as not to disturb his slumber. After the operation was complete, the man curled up in his improvised bed without realizing that his shoes had been taken with impunity.

Hayex now had to overcome the obstacle of introducing his large feet into the Greek's shoes. He tried and tried, and then he finally forced his feet to conform to the shoes. He tried to move his enormous toes, but they seemed to refuse such a painful procedure. Meanwhile, Califax tried very hard to disguise the attacks of laughter that the grotesque spectacle invoked. Several rings of smoke escaped from his nose, and he covered his snout with his claws to muffle his laughter. After a few minutes, Hayex was able to stand in the shoes, but not without complaining about how small the man's feet were. He took a few steps in those shoes and his walk proved more comical than his appearance. Califax could no longer contain his laughter: Hayex walked like a duck, which suffered from severe arthritis. Hayex covered himself with the cape, so that you could only see his large eyes. He was ready to undertake his risky venture.

"We should copy the inscriptions of the medallion on a piece of wood," suggested the gargoyle.

"It seems like a good idea to me. Thus, we will not expose the Key," agreed Califax.

Armed with a copy of the medallion, and the shoes and cape of the villager, the gargoyle went into the uncertain and dangerous world of men.

Walking on the crowded streets close to the market in Athens, Hayex drug the cape behind him along with the fear of being discovered by the humans. However, they seemed to care more about their own personal businesses than the small, odd creature in their midst.

The throngs of people made it difficult for the gargoyle to orientate himself. He rambled among the vast number of stands that offered diverse products from all over the world: silks from China, perfume from Egypt, spices from India and Africa, imposing weapons from Turkey, olive oil from Iberia and even exotic animals among many other choices of merchandise. He had never been so close to that many humans. He was fascinated by all the different kinds of merchandise, and he took extra time to satisfy his curiosity.

At one of the stands, a merchant hawked his wares. The aroma of the barbecued lamb, which the retailer cooked in large clay pots, drew Hayex. Hypnotized by that aroma, he stopped before the smooth and juicy meat that the salesman showed proudly to the passers-by in the market. To Hayex, seeing this meat cooked, displayed and offered in front of his face seemed as wonderful as the most outlandish fantasy of a shipwrecked sailor.

A large number of villagers were crowded around the stand, burying Hayex in an ocean of togas, gowns, and sandals of diverse color and design. In spite of his fear, the gargoyle was patient and waited for some scraps of meat to fall from the hands of the humans. After a short wait, he collected a goodly amount of meat that the men had wasted.

When he tried to escape all that hungry turmoil, he found that one of the villagers was standing on the cape that served as his veil. He tried to free himself by tugging and pulling, but the great weight of the fat man made his attempts to escape useless.

Remembering the words of Califax in the labyrinth of Lugh, he kept his calm. He had an idea that would help him get out of this jam. He pinched the leg of his oppressor with one of his claws. The villager jumped, releasing the cape, and shouted obscenities and winced from the pain of the gargoyle's pinch.

"Sir, if you do not like my product, you do not have to announce it in that manner!" the merchant protested, while the fat man leaped and jumped in pain.

That jumping mass opened a passageway in the crowd because he threatened to squash any and all that obstructed his path. Hayex took advantage of this time to abandon the stand with the food hidden under his cape. Once out of danger, on an abandoned street, he eagerly devoured that delicious lamb.

After that bittersweet experience, the gargoyle continued on the mission that had been entrusted to him. He returned to the market and began looking for the person who could help him decipher the strange inscriptions on the medallion.

After walking around the plaza for a few minutes, he approached one of the stands where a solitary sleepy merchant was seated in the shade of an improvised roof. The gargoyle approached the stand cautiously and, hiding his claws under the cape, deposited the piece of wood on the counter. The retailer spiritedly left his stupor when hearing that noise.

"Come in, young man! What can I do for you? I have a great variety of fish from the Corinth, from the Aegean Sea, the Ionian and the Mediterranean," he announced in a loud voice, in perfect Greek.

Hayex did not understand one word the merchant said, and only managed to point out the piece of wood that he had placed on the counter.

"Ichthus?" said the merchant, after reading the sign on the wood.

Meanwhile, Califax nervously walked circles around a tree because of the long absence of his companion. It had now been several hours. After a few minutes more, the gargoyle appeared with a cold and unexpected cargo.

"But... What is all this?" inquired Califax.

"I asked a man at one of the market stands and this was his answer," he justified his actions.

"But, why have you brought all this fish?"

"They are cheap and very good quality," he said, showing the finer traits of the product. "In addition to, he sold them to me on credit!" he announced.

"Are you crazy?" he snapped. "You did not go to buy fish, but to find out what the inscription of the Key means," he reprimanded.

"The merchant said *Ichthus* and then gave me all these fish. I had to come back here to unload the merchandise," he explained a little bit ashamed. "I could not resist the offer!" he admitted.

"Ichthus? That is to say that he could read the inscription," the dragon reflected while pacing back and fourth. "Do you know where the merchant is from?"

"I did not understand a word he said, but I think he was Greek," he clarified. "I am not very sure," he emphasized while he took off his disguise.

"Wait a moment! If the man is Greek and he could read the inscription, then *Ichthus* means fish, in Greek. That is why he gave you the fish," he speculated.

"Perhaps," agreed Hayex, uninterested, while he ate a fish.

"Do you remember what Dee the Magician, said? *The fish is the fisherman and his dwelling is in the east sea, where the cross came from to join with the sun.*"

"Yes, I remember," he answered with indifference, while he continued eating.

"Lets see, if the fish is the fisherman and the fish is *Ichthus*, then *Ichthus*, has to be the fisherman," Califax reasoned, starting his march from one side to the other again.

"It is possible," agreed the gargoyle.

"We do not know who the fisherman is, but according to Dee the Magician, he lives in the same place where the cross comes from, in the east sea. The pythoness said something similar."

"Then, perhaps we can find it in Judah, the place indicated on the Roman map," said Hayex.

Thus, the intrepid adventurers headed off for the biblical region of Palestine, crossing the archipelago of the Aegean Sea. Flying over the islands, they reached Naxos and the famous island of Patmos, where Saint John wrote the mysterious Book of Revelations.[61] When approaching the island of Rhodes, Hayex, alluding his grandfather, told of an enormous bronze statue that greeted the ships that passed by that way. He also said that it crashed to the ground in an earthquake.[62] In the Mediterranean, the adventurers reached the south coast of the island of Kypros,[63] where they could make out the Palestine shoreline. In those legendary lands, the dragon and the gargoyle initiated a new and exciting phase of their bold passage.

It is hard to be certain at this point of the story, but things, as time passed, became more difficult for the adventurers to obtain their objectives in this dangerous mission. The entire *Region of Fire*, and the lives of its inhabitants, depended on the boldness and intelligence of the young dragon.

---

[61] Apocalypse (Doctors note).
[62] The Colossus of Rhodes. One of the seven wonders of the ancient world. A statue 32 meters high that celebrated the deity Apollo. Erected by Chares the sculptor in 290 B.C. An earthquake destroyed it in 223 BC. (Doctors note).
[63] Cyprus. *Cuprum*, in Latin, which means copper. (Doctors note).

The Secret of the Dragon

5

The Fish and the Fisherman

IN THE REGION OF FIRE, THE DRAGONS CONTINUED to breath flames on matters without mercy. Operation "Defense Wall" had not prevented the Selenex raids on Dragonia's soil. The suspicions that there was a traitor in the Court of Helenex, led the King to designate Tradux, as a Head of the Intelligence Agency, in order to discover, as soon as possible, so disloyal courtier.

Meanwhile, in the comfort and intimacy of her cave, Darta read another one of the letters that Califax had written before leaving on his mission.

Even though Novax had fought to ease his intuitive wife, she could not stop worrying about the absence of her beloved little offspring.

"I have a feeling that my little one is distressed Novax," she said, with pleading eyes.

"I do not see why. Read his letters again. He is learning a lot and having fun in Amerux," Novax lied.

"I know, my love, but something tells me he feels lonely and disoriented," she explained, worried.

"Do not worry, my dear," he said embracing her lovingly. "Soon he will be with us," he assured her.

"It is what I want most, my love," said Darta, curling up lovingly in the arms of Novax.

Califax and Hayex flew on a southeastern course the Phoenician beaches of A-Jumhuriya al-Loubnaniya,[64] dominated by the frightful Persian Empire. Entering via the extensive Syrian Desert, through the beautiful city of Tarabulus,[65] the intrepid travelers turned towards the south following the slopes of the mountains of Jabal Loubnan. The mound founded in this immense oasis was covered with imposing cedars 120 feet high, which made up a vast forest that seemed as beautiful as the Persian carpet that inspired Scheherazade to tell a story to his sister Dinarzade.[66]

They crossed the Litani River, close to the city of Sidon, until they reached the rocky Tiro, and from there, they flew to the east, towards the Sea of Galilee.

---

[64] Lebanon: The Switzerland of East. (Doctors note).

[65] Present Tripoli, coastal city of Lebanon. (Doctors note).

[66] Scheherazade the Sultan told his sister Dinarzade a different story every night she requested. These later became the collection of Arab stories: *The Thousand and One Nights*. (Doctors note).

After a while, they could see a distant reflection of the Galilean sea, and the adventurers decided to take a rest in a desert area close to the city of Tiberias.

Hayex, decided to extinguish the thirst that had been oppressing him so long, he drank some water from a near spring.

"Yuck! This water tastes horrible!" exclaimed the gargoyle, making a repulsive facial gesture.

"These waters also contain sulfur," informed Califax after taking a swig. "Drink a little. I told you it is good for your health," he reminded.[67]

"These waters taste as repugnant as the ones in Italy," he complained.

"Do not be so sensitive, my friend, or you will die of thirst," replied the dragon, in a parental tone.

Night fell and the adventurers decided to look for a refuge where they could spend the night. The desert landscape did not offer many options. After a few hours of searching, they found a narrow cave in the slope of a mountain.

In spite of bitter experiences in the dark places where destiny had brought them, they went cautiously into that cold cavity. The fate that was in store for them required all their strength and intelligence, and even though they had to endure the discomfort that the hideout offered, Califax and Hayex slept like little newborn babies.

When the sun of the dawn rose, the dragon and the gargoyle devised a plan that they had to establish in

---

[67] The sulfuric waters of Tiberias were due to the nearby sulfur springs in the city of Hammat. (Doctors note).

order to follow through with the next stage of the mission. They would have to be more careful, since the sandy panorama in Galilee did not offer many places to hide from the wrath that fear evoked man.

After discussing it for quite a long time, the adventurers devised a scheme that would allow them to approach men without feeling threatened by them. Califax would disguise himself as a camel and Hayex his cameleer. In order to achieve this, Califax would use a costume to hide his royal self, under a blanket that covered his face and body, walking on his four feet and being very careful not to show his long tail, while Hayex would do his thing, just as he had done at the market in Athens. The gargoyle then went out to find a blanket large enough to cover the dragon and a new pair of shoes for himself.

In an orchard filled with olive trees, Hayex found a Roman Soldier who slept barefoot under the shade of one of those prized trees. What would be difficult, this time, was the fact that the soldier lay upon the blanket using it as a sort of mattress. Then the gargoyle used his great imitation abilities. He approached that loafer and in a soft and mysterious tone, he whispered in his ear: "*Get up; your time has come.*" When he heard that voice, the man woke up disturbed. Afterwards, Hayex immediately jumped in front of him with crazed eyes and sticking out his tongue, giving a tremendous scare to the man. The man shot out of there like an arrow, exclaiming incessantly: "*Satan! Satan!*"[68]

---

[68] Hebrew word meaning *Enemy*. Name with which it is also known Lucifer. (Doctors note).

"Satan? Who would that be...?" the gargoyle asked with surprise.

Watching at the man as he left, humorously, the place, Hayex hurried to seize the roman's blanket, boots and belt. He returned to the hide out where the dragon was waiting.

The design was not of Califax's taste, however given the difficulties they would have to go through to obtain another one, he accepted it. However, the blanket was not long enough to cover his enormous body, so they employed the saurian's royal cape as well.

"But, it is the cape that Rasux used to swear me in as the *Grand Dragon of the Chalice*," he protested.

"If we do not find the Chalice soon, you will be the *Grand Dragon of the Clowns*," refuted Hayex.

Califax hid his tail placing it on his back and tying it around his body with the Roman's belt, and once he was covered with the cloth and cape, which luckily covered his claws, the dragon looked like a huge camel with one large hump. Hayex covered himself with the cape he had obtained in the Athens market and he used the pair of Caligae [69] that he had recently acquired.

Hidden under their disguises, the daring travelers entered the Biblical region of Judea. Falling prey to great nervousness, they approached the beach on the Sea of Galilee to ask for the man they were looking for.

"Excuse me, Sir. I am seeking a man called *Ichthus*. Do you know where I can find him?" he asked rubbing his claws together nervously under cape that covered them.

[69] Boots that Roman soldiers used. (Doctors note).

"¿Ichthus? Who could have such a ridiculous name?" inquired the man.

"Is the fish the fisherman?" insisted Hayex.

"What kind of dull joke is this? I have never seen a fish with a net, boy," responded the man, with an outburst of laughter while he walked away.

Without losing spirit, they continued their search all along the coast of the lake. Later after several hours, they found a man close to Capharnaum, who told them, "The fisherman, who walked on these waters, is no longer with us. The fish was sacrificed in Jerusalem."

They returned to the refuge to wait for nightfall before flying towards Jerusalem, to track the last clue that that man had given them. Once the moon illuminated the desert, they followed the Jordan River until arriving to the north coast of Lake Asphaltites,[70] where they drank of its waters.

"Yuck! These waters taste worse than the ones in Italy!" said Hayex, throwing the water from his claws.

"You are right," agreed Califax. "They are too salty. How can men drink from it?"

They continued towards the west flying close to the city of Hircan, and arrived at the walled city of Jerusalem, where they got a glimpse of the fabulous Temple of King Solomon.[71] There, at dawn, they used the same plan they had used in Tiberias.

---

[70] Dead Sea. (Doctors note).

[71] King Solomon constructed the first temple around the year 1000 B.C. Destroyed in 587 B.C. by Nabuconodosor, King of Babylonia; Ciro, King of Persia reconstructed it. In the year 20 B.C. Herod destroyed it in order to construct his own version of the temple and in the year 70 A.D. the Romans destroyed it. Presently The Dome of the Rock is located there. (Doctors note).

The burning hot sun of the east came up on the desert steppe, when the adventurers began to plan on how they were going to find the slippery man called "Ichthus". Putting on their disguises, early that morning, they entered the city, crossing the valley of Kidron, and as veteran travelers, they walked the streets in search of a clue that would lead them to their destiny.

As the day passed, the city summoned up life, filling it with boisterous retailers and many consumers eager to buy different types of merchandise. The lofty streets of the city began to take its toll on the feet of the travelers, a price paid for walking on its dry footpaths.

"We have been walking for hours and these boots are killing me," complained Hayex profusely.

"And you think I am comfortable under these covers? I am dying of heat, my friend," replied an agitated Califax.

Close to the viaduct that crossed the city, they found a cistern that water was fed to from the Spring of Gihon,[72] where men and animals satiated their thirst. They walked quickly toward that urban oasis, anxious for the vital and refreshing liquid. Hayex's natural instinct betrayed him as he lay in front of the pool to drink the clear waters with his snout.

"Hey, boy!" exclaimed a man, disgusted by Hayex's actions. "Do not drink like the animals," he reprimanded. "Take this earthen bowl. What kind of education have your parents given you?"

[72] Spring located on the western slope of the Valley of the Kidron. (Doctors note).

Hayex had to learn to drink from the earthen bowl, while Califax had to learn to drink like a camel, to which a dragon of his ancestry and education was not accustomed.

After satisfying their thirst, the tired wanderers continued with their investigation. When they arrived to an esplanade in the ruins, they found a man who seemed to be writing down his observations. They approached him and the gargoyle asked.

"Could you help me, Sir? My name is Hayex and I am looking for a man called *Ichthus*," he said, hiding his face under the cape.

"My name is Solomon, disciple at the Flavius Josephus historical school.[73] I do not know anyone with that name. In fact, that word means fish, in Greek, son," clarified the scribe, in a friendly tone.

"Does *the fish is the fisherman* mean anything to you, Sir?"

"Now that you mention it, Josephus the teacher wrote something regarding this," he remembered, rubbing his beard. "The first Christians used a symbol similar to a fish to identify each other and to escape the persecution of Nero,"[74] he explained, reflectively.

"Christians?" asked Hayex, glancing furtively at the dragon.

"The followers of the Nazarethian, son," the historian clarified in a friendly manner.

"I do not know him, Sir."

---

[73] Notable Jewish historian who lived between 37 and 100 A.D. (Doctors note).

[74] Emperor Nero accused the Christians falsely and unjustly for the great fire of Rome. (Doctors note).

"They call him *The Christ*, that means *The Anointed One*, in Greek.

The gargoyle could only shrug his shoulders and the scribe continued.

"Many centuries ago, He preached in these lands, and one of his disciples betrayed him. The Sanhedrin condemned him and Pontius Pilate crucified him, but his followers said he revived and he went to Heaven," he informed.

"How is that possible?" Hayex asked, incredulously.

"How should I know? I do not believe in that. I only believe in Jehovah, Blessed be His name! He has the power," exclaimed the scribe.

"But, then, who am I looking for, teacher?" he asked, crossing his arms.

"There is an acrostic in Greek that means: *Jesus Christ, Son of God, Our Savior*. The initials of each of these words form *Ichthus* in the Greek language. Thus, the first Christians drew a fish so that others would know, in a discreet manner, that they were followers of Jesus of Nazareth," he explained, drawing a simple figure of a fish in the sand.

"Then, *Ichthus*, is the Roman god?" he asked, remembering the inscription that they saw on the cross in Saint Deiniol, in Bangor.

"Jesus Christ is, officially, the God of the Sacred Roman Empire of the East, since Constantine the First came to power, my friend," he informed.

Califax listened carefully to the words of the historian, hidden under his disguise. The mysterious words of Dee the Magician and the pythoness at Delphi, began to make sense. Then, with a slight push on Hayex's back, he urged him to continue asking questions.

"It seems that your camel wants to know more, son," said the scribe, after perceiving that gesture.

"Do not pay any attention to him. He is an inopportune ruminant," Hayex pretended to make excuses for the dragon as he looked at him with disgust.

"Would you like to know more, Hayex?"

"Yes, teacher. There is a legend about a Sacred Chalice. Do you know anything about it?"

"It would be better if you come with me, my friend," inviting him cordially. "It delights me when young people like you, are eager for knowledge of our great history. Perhaps, we can find something regarding this matter in our archives," he said taking the gargoyle by the shoulder pleasantly, while the dragon and the gargoyle looked at each other discreetly without really knowing what to do. Without options other than the one that presented itself here and now, they were directed to the heights of Jerusalem, following their unexpected guide.

Located to the west of the city, in a large house close to Harrods Palace, Hayex and Solomon entered a room that lodged the great library of the historian. Solomon explained that his collection came from diverse parts of the world, and that it had been assembled over the centuries by the intrepid hands of men and women who, with self sacrificing patience, dedicated a major part of their lives collecting information of man's everyday life in the altar of knowledge. Several parchments come from Rome, Egypt, Greece and many other nations, to saturate the shelves of that incredible Judean library.

With sincere and disinterested hospitality, the scribe offered a refreshing cup of red wine to his heat-exposed guest.

"Please, get comfortable, my young friend. The weather is very warm and you must be weary of that cape covering your face," he said, while he served some dates, honey and bread on a copper tray. The solitary idea of discovering his face sent great fear into Hayex's heart. He had to think quickly to come up with something plausible that would justify a refusal to such an invitation. He did not want Solomon to confuse him with that *Satan*, from whom the roman soldier ran away on, the day before. Meanwhile, Califax, who was following his companion's investigation from one of the windows, was alarmed by that suggestion and so he sent several smoke hoops from his nose.

"It is part of my ritual of initiation, teacher. I cannot reveal my face until it is concluded," Hayex lied with a tremulous voice.

"Ritual of initiation?" inquired Solomon.

"It is the formation phase of the *Bards*," he explained, while he ate the food from the tray.

"Bards?" questioned the historian, with professional curiosity.

"The Bards are aspiring students of the Druids, high priests of the Celts."

"Very interesting, Hayex," he said, taking a pen, ink and a piece of papyrus. "I know that the Celts are great soldiers and that they trade with the Greeks, but tell me, Where is your fascinating country?" he asked with interest, getting ready to write the gargoyle's words down, like a curious reporter.

"The Celts are based in many regions, but my village is in Briton, to the north of Europe."

Upon hearing that story, Solomon went to a shelf in the library where he brought down a papyrus and then he began to read. The document spoke of a Jewish man who was a distinguished member of the Sanhedrin and a supporter of Jesus, who traveled to the north of Europe, some time after the crucifixion of the Nazarethian.

"Joseph of Arimathea left Jerusalem, and according to some sources, he took with him a Saxon soldier's sword[75] and Jesus' Grail."

"Grail?" he inquired, intrigued, while he drank the wine from the cup.

"The Christians designate the Chalice, the one that Jesus drank from as the *Holy Grail*."

"Which means I have traveled all this way in vane?" he exclaimed.

"No, I do not think so, Hayex. Surly you have learned many things throughout your trip."

"What does the Chalice look like, teacher?" he asked, increasingly interested in Solomon's words.

"The papyruses do not mention it," he said, coiling the roll, "but it is well known that Joseph of Arimathea loaned his house to Jesus on the Passover previous to his crucifixion. Joseph's being a rich man makes it possible the Chalice is made of fine gold or bronze. However, despite that fact, Jesus was a simple man who never liked luxurious things. Jesus was the son of a carpenter, so it could have been a Chalice made of an olive tree wood."

---

[75] Property of a Roman soldier, probably obtained in a battle in the northern campaigns of Europe. (Doctors note).

"Why would he take the sword of a Saxon soldier too, teacher?" Hayex begged.

"The documents say that a guard cut into the body of Jesus with the sword while he was passing away on the cross. The Christians also consider it sacred," he explained.

"I have a copy of the Sacred Key. Do you know what the inscriptions mean?" he said, taking it out from under his cape.

The Sacred Key
(Obverse)

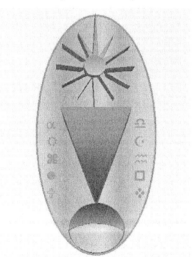

"I am the Alpha and the Omega; the Day and the Night; the Earth and the Water; Life and Death; the Sign and the Path," he said, solemnly, translating the hieroglyphics.

"Who could be so powerful, teacher?"

"Only Jehovah, Blessed is His Name! He is omnipotent," he exclaimed, lifting his hands to the sky.

"What significance does the medallion have, teacher?" the gargoyle continued his questioning.

"The group forms a type of cup, and its contour seems like a fish, but looking at it closely, its base is a moon in its first quarter, and its body seems to join the star with the moon," he said as he examined it. "It seems to say *the day emanates at night, and the night of the day*. One does not exist without the other. It is very interesting. Where did you get this copy?" he asked of the gargoyle.

"It is a long story. Perhaps, I can tell you on another occasion," he explained.

"In addition, the star has twelve points, Hayex," observed Solomon. "It could evoke the Twelve Tribes of Israel or, possibly the Twelve Apostles of Jesus. On the other hand, the reverse side has *Ichthus* written on it, which means fish in Greek," he said.

"That is why I have been looking for a man called *Ichthus*, teacher," he clarified.

"I see. This object is a type of key that leads to the Sacred Chalice of Jesus, and without a doubt, is the Holy Grail of the Christians," he affirmed.

"Where do you think I can find it, teacher?" asked the gargoyle.

"I do not know, for sure, son," he said, shrugging his shoulders. "After the crucifixion, the Sanhedrin jailed Joseph of Arimathea for providing a tomb for Jesus. They say that he was in prison for more than a year without food or water."

"How could he survive for so long, teacher?" he asked intrigued.

"They say that a dove provided water and food for him during all that time by means of the Grail. However, I find it more plausible that friends helped him during his confinement. Later, he fled to Ramat.[76] I know someone there who will be able to give you more information regarding the matter. His name is Nathan and he is a good man, although he is hard to get along with. He has many documents, but you must have patience with him," he advised.

"How can I thank you for your advice?"

"It is not necessary, Hayex. *Who kindly sets a wand'rer on his way does e'en as if he lit another's lamp by his. No less shines his, when he his friend's hath lit.*[77] However, I would request one thing of you. When you find the Chalice, tell me the story," he asked, amicably.

"Of course, teacher. You will be the first to hear it," he assured.

After having listened to Solomon the teacher, Hayex met up with his overheated companion to rest and then to go to the city of Ramat, where they would find more clues that could lead them to the Chalice.

The adventure seemed to have no end, but their objective was closer than ever to being achieved.

[76] Ramat Gan, northwest of Jerusalem. (Doctors note).
[77] Quintus Ennius, quote by Cicero's *De Officiis,* Book I of *Moral Goodness.* (Doctors note).

The Secret of the Dragon

6

The Apostle of the Grail

I N A DARK GROTTO NEAR THE TOWN OF RAMAT, THE reddish cupola of the Eastern dusk, welcomed the intrepid travelers who, tired of wandering, took a well deserved rest before resuming their adventure the following day. While Hayex slept like a log, Califax began to feel the implacable pain and nostalgia of being far from his family and home. He took the reliquary locket that his mother had given him from his long neck, and after looking at it for several minutes, his mind was flooded with pleasing memories. The melodious songs that formerly fell on his ears lovingly in his cradle when his mother would sing him to sleep, they seemed so near to him that he could almost hear them. On having looked at the shining sword that with great honor he received from the claws of his father, the day that he was undressed as *Great Dragon of the Chalice*, it evoked the games and escapades that, along with his brothers, easy prey of his progenitor was doing.

The night passed, afflicted by silence. The silver plated witness that illuminated the desert steppe intensified in brilliance when watched through the tears that welled in the young dragon's eyes.

The cock's crow announced the arrival of a new day and the globetrotters got ready to start their journey. Since the fauna around the place was scarce, they had to assault a fig tree, whose fruits they ate for their breakfast.

Disguising themselves again as camel and cameleer, they went to the village of Ramat to meet Nathan, friend and colleague of Solomon. The small population of Ramat contrasted with the hustle and bustle of Jerusalem, and the dusty streets seemed to intensify the heat that already scorched the legs of the two detectives, even though the day had just begun. Upon arriving at the southern part of the village, they walked toward a simple house that rose slightly above the rest of the structures, almost as if wanting to escape from the prying eyes of neighbors. Hayex knocked firmly on the door, and after a few minutes, a very tall, old man, white long wet hair and a thick white beard, crossed the threshold of the door.

"Who the devil comes to my door to annoy me at this hour of the morning?" he demanded in a powerful voice, as he violently flung opened the inner door to the house.

"Excuse me, Sir. I am looking for Nathan the teacher," said Hayex, with a tremulous voice.

"Eh? Who the heck are you?" he inquired as he towered over the short stature of the gargoyle.

"My name is Hayex and I have been sent by Solomon, the teacher, of Jerusalem," he explained.

"Does Solomon have nothing better to do other than to send me young lads like you?" he reproached, in a tantrum.

"I am sorry, Sir. I did not want to bother you, but it is very important that I speak with you," he insisted.

"I did not mean to be discourteous, son," he apologized, smoothing his voice. "It is only that I was bathing when you knocked at the door," he explained while he dried his hair with a towel.

Hiding his face under the cape, Hayex told his reasons for dropping in unexpectedly. The teacher looked distrustfully at the gargoyle from head to toe, and invited him to enter into that very old residence.

Anticipating the scribe's questions, he gave the same explanation about his clothes that he gave to Solomon, but Nathan seemed uninterested in his clothing and proceeded to serve him a glass of wine to the unexpected guest at his table.

"So, do you want to know where the Chalice is, eh? No one knows, son. After being released, Joseph went to the island of Cyprus. This is known because of the letters that he wrote to Nicodemus, another distinguished member of the Sanhedrin who also sympathized with the Nazarethian."

"Do you know why Joseph of Arimathea traveled to the west?" asked Hayex.

"Many say that he did so to escape the wrath of Saul of Tarsus,[78] who was a ferocious persecutor of the Christians before becoming one himself while on a trip to Damascus. Others say that he went to preach the Gospel to the pagans under instructions by Jesus himself. Many call him *The Apostle of the Grail*," indicated Nathan.

"The Gospel?" asked, Hayex, with interest.

"The Word of Jesus!" he scolded. "Joseph himself assured that he saw the Nazarethian resurrected, that is why he believed in Him," he explained.

"Is it true that Jesus was resurrected?" he asked, embarrassed.

"You do not believe in those things, do you? Only Jehovah has this power! Blessed is His Name!" he shouted as he spread his arms wide as if to encompass the whole sky.

"Of course not!" he agreed with surprise. "It would be better if I were on my way, teacher. I need to travel to Cyprus," he said, getting up from the table.

"When you get to the island, Hayex, go to Nicosia," he advised. "Surely, you will find someone there to help you. The place is plagued with Christians."

With the sun on their backs, they flew on a course to the Mediterranean and the Island of Cyprus. The clues that the Judean teachers had given them brought them closer to their goal. However, they were far from imagining the vicissitudes with which they would have to deal.

[78] Saint Paul (Doctors note).

They arrived at Nicosia, capital city of Cyprus that, at that time, was shared by the Romans and the Turks.[79] They hid in the thickness of the trees on a hill near the city. They planed their strategy in order to continue with their search.

This time, the idea was to enter the city at dusk, when it was easier to hide their identity to those inquisitive eyes of men.

There was a river of swirling languages, cultures and religions on the crowded streets of Nicosia, where Turks, Greeks and Romans intermingled. The daring travelers wandered these streets and found a Christian church, where a parish priest, in turn, celebrated the mass of the afternoon to the faithful followers of Jesus. They waited for the mass to end, after which Hayex spoke with Father Constantius, a short plump man with little hair who dressed in a funeral black tunic.

"Excuse me, teacher. My name is Hayex, and I would like to know if you could help me," he inquired in a low voice as he approached the pulpit of the sacred enclosure.

"Of course, my son. You are in the house of God," he said, inviting the gargoyle to sit on one of the benches. "How can I help you?" asked the clergyman, in an amicable tone.

"I am following the footsteps of Joseph of Arimathea. I would like to know where he went after he left Jerusalem."

---

[79] It was not till 688 A.C. that Justinian II, emperor of the East, signed a treaty with the Caliph Abd-al-Malik, but in 695 A.C., Leontius, overthrew Justinian. However, the treaty lasted almost 300 years before Nicephorus Phocas expelled the Turks in 965 A.C. (Doctors note).

"Joseph of Arimathea?" he inquired. "That happened six centuries ago, son. Nevertheless, certain registries indicate to us that he left this island on course to Briton[80], north of Europe. But, tell me: what is your interest in all this, my son?" the priest asked, intrigued, resting his back heavily on the support of the bench.

"I must find the Sacred Grail of the Christians, teacher," revealed the gargoyle, innocently.

"The Grail?" he inquired, getting up from the bench. "It is a sacred relic and nobody knows where it is, son, but I will tell you this, only one pure of heart can see it. I suggest that you desist from your pretensions. If your faith is sincere, you do not need to have the Grail in your hands," he preached, turning his back on him while rubbing a crucifix.

"But it is very important that I find it, teacher. The survival of a nation depends on it," he explained, without measuring his words.

"What nation are you talking about?" he inquired again, aiming an accusing look at the gargoyle. "Who are you, ungodly creature of the darkness?" demanded the parish priest, angrily, while approaching the interlocutor slowly.

Hayex, surprised by the sudden rage of the priest, wanted to flee as soon as possible from that place, but in his haste, he tripped over another one of the benches in the church. The Father reached for him, yanked the cape off his head, and looked into the gargoyle's terrified face.

---

[80] According to a legend, Joseph of Arimathea founded the first Christian church in the first century A.C., in Glastonbury, where it was built one of the most important abbeys in all of England up to the tenth century A.C. (Doctors note).

"Satan! Satan!" shouted the prelate at the top of his lungs, while he brandished the cross in his hands.

Hayex left the place hastily to meet up with Califax, who was waiting, impatiently, at the doors of the church. When he saw that his companion had lost his cape, he knew, then, that something had gone wrong. The gargoyle warned him of his complete failure while he mounted the dragon's back. Califax could not fly because his wings were still tied for the disguise, so he galloped through the streets of the city toward the refuge oh hills. Meanwhile, Father Constantius attacked the *diabolic* fugitives with all manner of improper language. To make things worse, a crowd of villagers seemed to appear from out of nowhere and as is always in the case when fear and ignorance rule, united with the preacher's unsubstantiated cause.

Thus, the intrepid adventurers miraculously escaped from Nicosia, but not without unjustly maligned by its god-fearing inhabitants.

They removed their disguises and caught their breath under the protection of the dark night. Califax debilitated by his frantic race from the village, collapsed like a tree on the fresh grass of the prairie. Once he caught his breath, the anxious saurian asked Hayex what had happened in the recent occurrence inside the church.

"The man discovered me, but I was able to find out that the teacher Joseph went to Briton," he replied.

"It seems we are back where we started," said the dragon, discouraged. "Who can we ask in Briton?"

"Perhaps, we can approach the Magician, again. Do not you think?" inquired Hayex.

The copper-colored light of dawn announced a new day on the island of Cyprus, and the intrepid adventures flew on a course to Briton following the same route that had brought them to Judea. They flew over the Mediterranean until reaching the Aegean Sea and then crossed the Greek islands until they reached the boot-shaped Italian peninsula.

When they were over the Pennine Alps, the cold wind of the north started to chill the travelers to the bone. They had taken very little time to rest, and they felt the enormous load of the long and debilitating journey.

Traveling north, they decided to fly down to Neuchatel, the Swiss lake, in the region of La Tene,[81] to make a truce with their weary bones before continuing with the trip.

A sudden and violent snowdrift in the lower portion of the French Alps surprised them. The stormy wind that whipped at their faces hindered the adventurer's advance, and the icy cold forced them to stop and take refuge from the storm. Califax flew ahead of Hayex with the intention of examining the slope of a mountain. He found a cave where they could take refuge. Califax waited for his friend's arrival inside the grotto, but he became concerned when the gargoyle failed to arrive.

Outside, the storm got worse, as if its fury tried to rip the side of the mountain from its base. Califax was worried about the absence of the gargoyle. He waited a few minutes more and then decided search for him.

---

[81] Archaeological region that marks early Celtic civilization, developed between the V and the I centuries B.C., later to the developed in Austria, in the region of Hallstatt. (Doctors note).

In the middle of that impenetrable curtain of snow, the dragon called incessantly looking for his friend, but his shouting was muted by the storm, while he maintained an unfruitful battle against the intense cold. He continually sent out blazes of fire in hopes that his friend would see his position. In spite of his efforts, Hayex did not appear.

Night fell and the storm impetuously attacked the mountain. Califax had found no sign of the gargoyle. After searching for several hours, the dragon resigned himself to the fact that he would have to give up his search until the storm passed. He returned to the cave, cried for the loss of his friend, and waited for the storm to pass.

Dusk came with twilight on the horizon marking the end of the storm; the moon flirted timidly with the snowy summits of the imposing French Alps.

Alone and saddened inside the cave, Califax analyzed what had happened. He blamed himself for the misfortune of Hayex. Had he not flown ahead looking for a refuge in the mountains, Hayex would be with him now. "I should never have left him in the middle of that snow storm!" He admonished himself between sobs. In spite of the difficult weather conditions, the dragon decided to go outside to search, again, for his companion. Although he feared the worst, he could not leave him in the middle of that immense mountain range. He would at least have to take the cadaver to its native land.

Just as suddenly as the storm had arrived, the gray cloudy mantle quickly moved away revealing the pale rays of light from the beautiful full moon that illuminated the region. The soothing wind felt strange after the heavy attacks of the snowstorm. Califax was sure that the shinning of the stars in the firmament shared his pain with him in sorrow.

After anxiously rummaging around the slopes of the mountains for hours, Califax faced the sad reality. Hayex was congealed on the foot of a rocky crag, not very far from the cave where the dragon had taken refuge. Huge dragon tears spilled from his eyes and he gingerly lifted the frozen, inert body of his friend and carried him to the refuge.

"Why do you have this strange desire to become a statue, my friend?" he said crying, bitterly, while he warmed Hayex's body with a light flame.

Califax could not bear to see his friend in that lifeless state. He walked deeper in to the cave, as the heat changed the blue color of Hayex's skin to his normal, light brown, color. Califax sobbed and sniffled uncontrollably with grief.

"Why do you cry, my friend?" asked the voice.

"Because Hayex is dead," the young dragon responded automatically.

"What?" he asked, alarmed.

"It is true. I could not save him," the dragon explained. He was too stricken with grief over the loss of his friend to consider where the voice came from.

"Are you sure I am dead?" he inquired, touching him his own body.

"Hayex...? You are alive!" exclaimed Califax grabbing him up into a huge hug of happiness.

After that experience, they spent the night under the mute stare of the moon, and the stars gleamed now as if in some kind of a cosmic celebration.

On the following day, the morning sun awakened them, and the blue sky contrasted intensely with the stormy day before. The travelers continued their exciting trip with renewed spirit and strength.

They crossed the river basin of Paris until they reached the coast of Calais, in the French Gallia. Later they crossed the English Channel in route to the city of Canterbury.

After the long trip, they took a rest in a place close to the delta on the River Thames, very close to Londinium. They searched for something to fill their empty stomachs.

"This time let it be me who brings something for us to eat," said Califax, in a jovial tone.

"Very well. But promise me that you will not bring fish, this time," pleaded the gargoyle.

Walking in the thick of the forest, Califax found a group of men impatiently roasting an enormous wild boar on the fire. It seemed as thought they had recently hunted and killed it, and were now anxious to eat it. They looked like a group of Anglo-Saxon soldiers taking a rest after a long and tiring patrol. So, knowing the fear and wrath that he could instill in men, Califax climbed a huge tree, and letting himself fall quickly snatched the delectable roasting meat with his hind legs in mid flight right before the astonished eyes of those soldiers.

As they watched the frightful monster fly away with the day's food, the men shouted insults followed by the well-known and abominable epithet, *"Lucifer! Lucifer¡"*

Hayex could not contain his joy when smell of the roasted boar wafted under his nostrils. He could not stop thanking his loyal companion for the sumptuous dish that he eagerly wolfed down.

"I could not remember the taste of wild boar, my friend. Men know how to flavor the meat very well," observed Hayex. "I always ask myself what it is that they put on it to make it so delicious."

"I do not know, but it is exquisite," seconded Califax.

After the banquet and a well-deserved nap, they flew directly to River Dee, where they went into forest chamber of the mysterious Magician who, again appeared from the fog in a dramatic way.

"What do you want to know?" asked his visitors, in a friendly voice

"The teacher, Joseph of Arimathea, brought the Chalice to these lands. How can we find it, Sir?" quizzed the young dragon.

"The apostle deposited the Grail in the place where the moon completes two cycles. The tears of the tree of Myrddin will reveal the mystery when its light shines between the sun and the moon," he said, gravely.

Once again, Dee the Magician disappeared with the fog.

Califax and Hayex stood still looking at one another completely puzzled. The words of the Magician were more mysterious and difficult to interpret each time, and time was running out inexorably. In addition to finding the Chalice, they would also have to find the man who would activate its power.

They left that tenebrous forest, and deliberated regarding the Magician's riddle.

"We know that the tears of the tree of Myrddin are elektrons. On the other hand, it is possible that, *between the sun and the moon* means dusk or the dawn of the day. However, how are we going to spill the light of the elektron?" asked Califax.

"What does it mean: *Deposited the Grail in the place where the moon completes two cycles?*"

"I do not know. This riddle is truly difficult," answered Califax.

"How long does a moon cycle last?" Hayex asked, looking at the sky.

"Twenty-eight days, if I remember correctly," answered the dragon.

"That is peculiar! In Peel Dagda[82] there are twenty-eight stones positioned in a circle," informed the gargoyle, after meditating a bit.

"That is true, Hayex! Perhaps that it the answer, my friend!" exclaimed and exited Califax.

They left, for Peel Dagda at nightfall. They were unaware of the doom that loomed about them. The evil dragons waited only for the opportunity to take the Chalice from them and to give it to the traitor in Dragonia: these evil ones had been monitoring their every move.

They found that the enigmatic place was abandon, a fortunate circumstance which allowed them to explore the structure. They began to meticulously, examine the huge rocks.

[82] Stonehenge (Doctors note).

Peel Dagda was made up of two large circles. The majority of it was constructed out of twenty-eight perfectly aligned enormous stones, the inner construction comprised of ten huge monoliths formed in a smaller circle. The northern part of the inner circle had two stones with the hollows that they had seen before. The same hollows were present on the southeastern rocks, with one difference: the rocks were separated by a space that made up the entrance to the circle. The positioning and orientation of the rocks seemed to signal, principally the moon's path, as well as some other important stellar positions. Califax observed that, all the hollows were circular and more or less the size of a lime.

"Those hollows are probably the receptacles for the Myrddin tree tears. What do you think, Hayex?"

"That means we will have to find elektrons of the same size, my friend," answered Hayex.

"You said that you knew where to find a large number of them," reminded Califax.

Therefore, they departed for the forest where they found the prized oak ambers.

They gathered as many as they could and took them back to Peel Dagda. They sorted the ambers to choose the ones that would fit perfectly into the holes in the rocks. The daring adventurers did not know what to expect next.

"What do you think is to going to happen, my friend?" inquired Hayex.

"I do not know. The Magician, said: *The tears of the tree of Myrddin will reveal the mystery when its light shines between the sun and the moon*".

"And what of the Key...? Has its only purpose been to take us to the east and return us here?" he wondered aloud.

"The key! That is it, my friend!" exclaimed Califax, taking it out of his bag.

Remembering the observations of Solomon, the teacher, Califax explained to his friend that they must spill the light of the elektrons between the sun and the moon, which were engraved on the medallion.

"But, how are we going to do that?" asked Hayex.

"Perhaps, we should bring the medallion closer to the elektrons," he answered.

Arduous was the task of directing the light of the moon through the ambers and to the medallion. In addition, the work of the explorers was interrupted, since the moon constantly hid itself behind the clouds that moved across the sky. After several failed attempts, they took a breather. Disappointed, they sat leaning against one of the monoliths on the north side, while the canticle of the forest seized their imagination under the dark mantle of the looming black clouds. The phantom of failure unfolded its dark cloak on the sprit of the travelers once again. After several minutes of funeral muteness, Hayex interrupted the silence.

"Do you think that we were mistaken in our interpretation of Dee's message?" Hayex asked, downtrodden.

"It is possible, my friend," the dragon agreed disappointed.

Suddenly, the clouds in the sky separated and the moon illuminated the central esplanade of the temple. Then, Califax observed an intense brilliance that emanated from the floor. Intrigued by the luster, he approached to investigate followed by his faithful comrade. It was apparently a rocky needle shaped pyramidal nail with its four flanks splendidly polished.

"What do you think this is for?" Hayex asked intrigued.

"Let me try something," requested the dragon.

Next, Califax carefully placed the center of the backside of the Key over the point of the pyramid stone, and to his surprise, the medallion balanced perfectly. Shortly afterward, the dragon and the gargoyle witnessed a magical event that defied expression. The Key began to spin in the opposite direction to the hands of the clock at a speed that increased with every second. The astonished witnesses backed away before that strange phenomenon when a moon ray illuminated the amber in one of the stones on the east side, causing it to bounce off the Key and cause it to whirl at an even more dizzying pace. An instant later, the golden color ray of light traveled to the western side, and in turn cause a similar reaction in the rock on the north side and then returning to the Key. The ray then reflected off the other amber on the east and returned to the original amber, completing a passage that formed two triangles on a vertex that illuminated the interior of the temple with an intense golden glow.

The astonishment would not end with that exceptional play of lights. After several minutes of watching that impressive spectacle, they heard a strange noise coming from the exterior of the stony circles. Attracted by that sound, they quickly went outside and marveled at what they saw emanating from the 56 strange holes, they were beautiful circular silver plates, supported by a rod made of the same plated metal. Thirteen of those bases showed a beautiful chalice protected under a crystal cupola as splendid as a jewel.

Califax and Hayex could not help but be stupefied and, slowly they approached those yearned for chalices.

"This is incredible!" exclaimed the dragon.

"They are all beautiful, but which is the one we are looking for?" asked Hayex intrigued.

"The one that belongs to Jesus!" said the dragon.

"But, do you know which one belongs to Jesus my friend?" questioned the gargoyle.

Califax was doubtful for a few seconds but upon reflection, he said to the gargoyle.

"The teacher, Joseph of Arimathea, was a rich man. It must be this one. It's made of pure gold," he said pointing to one of the cups.

"However, a rich man could have bought a glass, silver, bronze, or maybe that exquisite ceramic one. What do you think?" cautioned Hayex.

"You are right, Hayex. Then, which one would be the one that Jesus drank from?" asked Califax.

"Remember, that Solomon said that Jesus was a simple man. So he could have used a wooden chalice," reasoned Hayex.

"However, Jesus was a King and I do not think he would use such material," said Califax.

"And I never knew a King whose followers ended up crucifying him. Everything is possible, my friend."

"Do you think it is that one?" reflected Califax taking his chin into his claw.

"Why don't we take them all?" suggested Hayex. "That way, we can be sure."

"It seems too easy to me. There must be a trick to all this," warned Califax.

"Perhaps, the light of the elektrons will direct us to the Chalice, my friend," hoped Hayex.

They went back inside the temple where the Key was still whirling and the golden lights continued to illuminate the place. After some time to watch them, they concluded that the light, formed a Grail, whose base pointed to the exit and the mouth to the chalice made of wood. So they went to the wooden chalice and slowly removed the protective shied from it. Califax secured in his claws. Next, the rest of the cups returned slowly to wherever they had come from, and the chance to gather the other chalices was gone.

"I told you there was a trick to all this, Hayex," preened the dragon, as he watched how they disappear into the depths.

Suddenly, an outcry tore at the night's silence. At short distance there was rising a formidable cloud of dust that was threatening to gobble the brave travelers, and there was no way to avoid it. It was a troop of Celtic soldiers who had discovered the presence of the intruders in that sacred enclosure.

Even though they hurried to pick up the Key, the determined adventurers lost valuable time that could have cost them dearly: their lives.

They took flight from the interior of Peel Dagda. As they lifted off the ground, the soldiers mercilessly sprayed the sky with arrows. One of them hit Califax's right wing and caused him to fall, resoundingly, in an open area of that solitary steppe. The men, knowing that they had wounded their prey, started the persecution. The swift horses devoured the distance that separated them from their prey, but just a few meters from the moment when they would have driven their weapons into the dragon, Hayex, valiantly, confronted them.

Suddenly, the men stopped in their tracks, turned and ran terrified, as if an imposing creature threatened to destroy them in one blow. Hayex swelled with pride and wiped his hands as if to say 'finished' when he saw how the soldiers scurried in panic. He turned to where his friend waited for him. Then he saw something that made him freeze in his tracks: two formidable figures that had been there behind his back all the time. A gigantic Pantesux dragon extended his claw to the perplexed gargoyle, who stammered:

"Who are you two?"

"I am Crulux and this is Dragax, guards at the royal court of Dragonia, my friend. Who are you?" he asked with a deep voice.

"I am Hayex, friend and comrade to Califax, the Grand Dragon of the Sacred Chalice," he proclaimed proudly in response to the friendly gesture of the saurian.

Hayex and his enormous companions quickly went to Califax's rescue. Califax was surprised to see these unexpected benefactors. Fortunately, the arrow did not hit any important veins and the membrane of his wing would heal quickly.

Crulux explained his presence saying that he was following his father's orders to patrol a large area of

Briton, together with other dragons. This mandate was in response to the preoccupation of Novax who wanted to know how his son faired.

Diagram of Peel Dagda
(View from above)

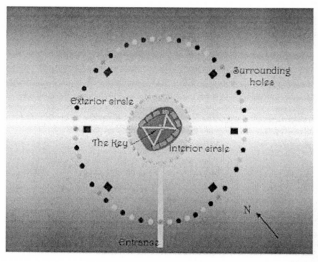

"In fact, our orders were to find your cadaver and return it to Dragonia," explained, Crulux, with frightening cold-heartedness.

"It seems as though it is not my time, yet, Crulux. Please, tell my father that I will soon bring what I promised him back to Dragonia," he declared.

"Will you be all right, Califax?" asked Crulux, amicably.

"Yes. Do not worry. Hayex will take care of me," he assured them.

"We will be in the area for a short time longer if you need anything," Crulux offered.

Crulux and Dragax took flight and their grey figures became indistinguishable from the immense darkness. After applying a mud patch to the wound of his friend, Hayex mad a comfortable bed for the dragon, safe in the woods. They took turns guarding the valuable treasure, which had cost them so much effort to find.

"You risked your life for me, my friend," thanked Califax.

"It was nothing. Crulux and Dragax were there all the time," clarified the gargoyle.

"That is true, but you did not know it when you stopped those men from harming me," Califax smiled a loving smile.

"It is the least that I could do for the one who saved my life," smiled Hayex as he tended to Califax's wound.

"What better than a mud expert to apply a mud patch?" Califax joked with a thankful smile on his snout.

The Secret of the Dragon

7

The Guardian of Ra

THE NIGHT WANED GIVING WAY TO THE LIGHT OF dawn. The brave globetrotters woke up from a deep and restful sleep. The recent disquieting events they had lived through, had not given them time to take a well-deserved and invigorating rest. Tracks of sleeplessness were reflected in their tired and ashen colored faces.

Califax inspected the wound on his wing and observed that it was healing well, but it was still not healed enough for him to fly.

"From what I can see, I will have to feed and take care of you," smarted Hayex.

"I hope I do not cause you too much trouble, my friend," smiled Califax.

With no other option than to go look for the day's food, the gargoyle walked towards the human dwellings. After a short time, he found a small farm.

Given his bitter past experiences on farms, he made sure the farmers were occupied in their daily work. He watched them from the safety of an enormous tree the trunk.

While he measured the time it took the land-owners to travel from place to place on the farm, in order to choose an opportune time sneak in and grab some food, a hand touched his back and he froze.

"What kind of a thing are you?" asked a small six year old girl, without any fear, almost scaring the gargoyle out of his wits.

His face turned the color of a snowflake. Hayex breathed a sigh of relief when he saw the little human girl. His regained his color and asked her:

"What is your name?"

"I am Udrie," she said in a tiny, melodic voice.

"My name is Hayex and I am a gargoyle. What are you doing here?"

"I am looking for my dear cat. I think he is lost," she explained with a worried look.

"A delicious cat?" said Hayex, licking his lips uncontrollably.

"What did you say...?" asked the little girl, alarmed at the gargoyle's behavior.

"That is, your precious cat, dear," he amended, with a false smile.

"Will you help me look for him?" asked the little girl, with a sweet smile.

"But of course, precious! What is your cat's name?" he exclaimed, rubbing his claws together, envisioning a cat morsel.

"His name is Linx and his fur is brown," Udrie said.

Motivated by different reason, the gargoyle and little Udrie went about the task of looking through the forest for the slinky cat.

Little Udrie walked deep into the forest shouting the name of her dear cat, and looking at the tops of the trees, since the feline routinely climbed to the top branches. Suddenly she tripped over a rock and fell to her knees. When she got up, she ran straight into Califax's imposing figure. He remained as still and quite as a statue with his back to the small girl, limiting himself only to listening to her movements.

Curious, as was to be expected, the little girl took the dragon by the tail and walked around to greet him face to face. She questioned him about his strange, to her, appearance. Califax explained in a soft and gentle voice, that he was a dragon from a distant land and that he was wounded.

"Poor Califax! You must be very hungry, is it not thus?" asked the concerned little girl.

"Yes, my dear, but my friend went out to look for something to eat."

"Is your friend a gargoyle?" she asked balancing herself on her heels, with on finger in her mouth.

"Yes. Perhaps you have seen him, dear?" he asked.

"He is helping me look for my cat that has lost his way," she explained naively.

"It would be better if we find Hayex before he finds your cat," he suggested, knowing what the gargoyle's true intentions were.

Califax joined Udrie to look for Linx, and after a few minutes of poking around the forest, they found the pussycat trapped in a branch of a tree being feverishly harassed by Hayex. With his hair standing straight up on his back and baring his teeth, the scared little cat spit and swatted at his relentless persecutor, who had very easily reached the feline's ineffective refuge.

"Linx!" exclaimed the little girl when she saw her darling cat.

Hayex had already caught it, but, from the moment he saw Califax and the little girl come into view, he also knew that he had jut lost his snack. He came down from the tree holding the frightened cat, and, having no choice, under the watchful eyes of the dragon, but to flash a sheepish smile and to gently hand the feline over to the little girl.

"Oh! Thank you, Hayex!" said little Udrie, while she gave him a smacking kiss on his gargoyle cheek that he later rubbed as if to remove the human kiss.

"It was nothing, dear child," said the gargoyle sheepishly.

As a grateful gesture, the little girl invited the hungry travelers to her house where she offered to feed them. They tried to explain to the child that adults were not usually friendly to strange guests.

Far from being discouraged by their refusal, little Udrie offered to bring, personally, the food to them. This offer was accepted with pleasure.

"Not all humans are bad," said Califax while watching the girl walk away with a bounce in her step.

After a while, the little one returned loaded with delicious roasted chicken and some large loaves of bread all of which that they devoured quickly.

"You were right, my friends!" she affirmed. "I told my mama about you, but she says that dragons and gargoyles do not exist."

"It is not important, dear. I did not believe that dragons existed either until I met Califax," clarified Hayex.

Over the following four days, Udrie continued to feed the bold adventurers. When Califax's wing had healed, they would be on their way to resume their adventure. The constant disappearance of food raised suspicions in little Udrie's home. Her mother was afraid that the little girl was feeding some wild animal, without knowing that the animal could put her life in danger. Armed with her stout husband, one afternoon she followed the little girl deep in the forest where Califax and Hayex were hiding. When they saw that their little girl was sharing food and conversing with those frightful beings, the woman expelled a scream no less terrifying than appearance of the dragon and the gargoyle. When the man saw that strange scene, he threatened them with a long lance in order to frighten them and move them away from his defenseless daughter.

"You see, Mama," she pointed. "Dragons and gargoyles do exist," the little one naively informed them.

Califax and Hayex remained petrified for a moment, but after that, they instinctively grabbed their valuable treasure and took to the air, verifying that the dragon's wing had healed.

Once in the air, the expeditionary adventurers took one last look at that family of humans. They noted the sobbing woman embracing her baby, Udrie. Little Udrie, waving her little hand at them, sent her last good-bye to her exceptional friends. Meanwhile, the man profaned unspeakable insults and terrible theatricalities in the general direction of those *'infernal invaders'* of his home.

They flew towards the north where they saw the gigantic horse of Uffington that was painted on the ground of that great landscape[83] where they took a rest. Later they flew to the mystical chambers of Dee the Magician. They had hoped that, the wise old Magician could give them clues on how to find the mysterious man whom they must deliver the Chalice.

After his customary theatrical appearance, the Magician made his inquiry in a deep voice:

"What do you want to know?"

"Where can I find the man to whom I must give the Chalice?" asked Califax.

"The guardian of Ra, the sun of the east, indicates the secret way to the Rock of Ebony," he intoned.

After those brief words, the Magician disappeared. The adventurers were perplexed. The words of the Magician resounded in their minds as if they had been spoken in some totally unknown dialect.

---

[83] Monumental horse 110 meters long and 40 wide. It was drawn scraping the surface of the ground leaving the chalk earth in the area uncovered. According to archaeological calculations, this figure dates back 2000 years. (Doctors note).

"Now, what do we do?" asked the gargoyle.

"We do not know any guardian of Ra, but it seems that we will be traveling to the east, again, Hayex."

They flew on a course to the beaches of Calais and crossed the Paris river basin, taking special care while entering the treacherous summits of the Alps. During this trip, the brave travelers only stopped to eat and sleep in the same places where they had traveled before. They would avoid the Oracle of Delphi by Califax's request.

They decided to pay a visit to Solomon, the teacher, in Jerusalem. To do so, they would have to disguise themselves again as camel and cameleer.

Once in the land of Palestine, they flew over the river basin of the Jordan River until arriving at the Sea of Galilee. They followed its channel and stopped shortly before reaching the Dead Sea. They turned towards the west on to Jericho, until reaching the outskirts of the sacred city of Jerusalem.

The night surrounded the Biblical metropolis with its poignant mantle, and the exhausted comrades let their tired bodies rest. They would not open their eyes again until the new day.

The crow of the rooster announced the new dawn, and the dragon and the gargoyle assumed their corresponding roles before visiting Solomon. The fight they both had with their respective clothing, took the better part of the morning, but before the sun reached its zenith, they were ready for work.

Walking on the stone streets of Jerusalem, they ran into an Arab merchant who offered to buy Hayex's camel. Surprised by that offer, the gargoyle had enough impudence to ask how many denarii's[84] he would offer for that *'ruminant'* who had fortunately made a great effort to hide his true identity by heavily shoving his bold *'cameleer'*.

"I think he is not for sale, Sir," said Hayex, upon feeling the shove from Califax. "It is a very special breed."

Only a short time had passed when the dragon upbraided for that insult. Hayex only laughed harder. He explained that even though it was a magnificent offer, he would not be capable of selling a friend. Shortly after noon, they reached the house of Solomon who with his customary hospitality received the gargoyle with an effusive greeting and a refreshing cup of wine, while Califax waited outside the house in the extreme heat of that region.

"I see that your initiation rite has not yet concluded," observed an amused Solomon upon since Hayex was still completely covered by the too warm robe.

"This is true, teacher. I still have a long way to go before I become a Bard."

"In arts and sciences, patience and perseverance are indispensable ingredients required to for success," He advised. "However, tell me, what measure of curiosity has brought you back to my humble dwelling? Have you found Jesus' Chalice?" he asked.

"We are working on that, but what has brought me back is a riddle that I have not been able to solve."

"Very interesting, my young friend! Tell me, Hayex, what is the question that incarcerates your thoughts?" he asked with interest.

[84] Currency made of silver, coined by the Romans. (Doctors note).

"Who is the guardian of Ra, the sun of the east?"

Rubbing his beard, Solomon went to his inseparable papyruses, from which he extracted all his great wisdom. He unrolled one of them and began to explain.

"Many centuries ago, Ramses II, the heartless Pharaoh of Egypt, enslaved my country. It was our father Moses who released us from his cruel yoke and guided us, over a span of 40 years, through the desert until we reached these lands: The Promised Land of Jehovah, Blessed be His name!" he exclaimed. "The construction of the pyramids would not have been possible without the unjust enslavement of the peoples of the weaker countries surrounding Egypt," he stated sadly.

"The pyramids?" he inquired, fascinated.

"The great pyramids of Egypt, in the region of Gizeh," he clarified. "They were constructed for the Pharaohs of Cheops,[85] Chephren and Mykerinus: each was buried there, with great honor, as if they were true gods."

"How very interesting, teacher. But, who is the guardian of Ra?" asked the Gargoyle.

"Be patient, my young friend," he said attempting to calm the gargoyle with a gesture of his hand. "The pyramids were constructed in such a way that their vertex aims towards Ra, god of the Sun, with whom the Pharaohs join in the next world," he said as he selected another roll from the shelf. "The Guardian of Ra is the Sphinx, the Great Lion that supposedly protects and watches over the mausoleum of the Pharaohs. In this papyrus," indicated Solomon, while unrolling it, "you can see its location and an image of the Sphinx as well as the pyramids.

---

[85] Called *Khufu* by the Greeks. (Doctors note).

"That is impressive, teacher. But why did the Egyptians build it?"

"In this site close to the pyramid of Chephren, you can read an inscription that says: *I protect the temple of your tomb and funeral chamber. I drive away enemy invaders and their military weapons at your will.*"[86]

"Does this mean that the Sphinx is the guardian of the Pharaohs?" he asked with surprise.

"It seems that way. Some explorers, Romans and Greeks, say that a secret passage exists within the Sphinx that leads to a chamber containing several prophecies inscribed on the walls."

"What do the prophecies say, teacher?" asked the gargoyle.

"Nobody knows. Not everyone, who has tried to profane the chamber by entering, has returned to tell the story, my friend."

The frightening memory of their incursion in the labyrinth of Lugh came to the gargoyle's mind right away. Meanwhile, Califax listened very intently to the words of the wise Solomon, while standing very next to the window of the house.

"However, tell me, what is your interest in all this Hayex?" asked the scribe.

"It is part of the search for the Chalice, teacher. I will tell you all about it when I finish," he promised.

"I'll be anxiously awaiting your tale. You have not forgot your promise to tell me the entire story, is it not so?" reminded Solomon.

---

[86] Site that dates to the time of Chephren, in the fourth dynasty, around 3100 B.C. (Doctors note).

"Of course not, teacher. You will be the first to know the story," assured Hayex.

Thus, Califax and Hayex traveled to mysterious Egypt, following the coast of the Mediterranean, until they reached the huge fan-like delta made by the Nile River, the longest in the world. The vast expanse oh the Nile as is bathed the countryside from Sinai to Alexandria left the bold travelers in awe of its greatness.

Night had fallen, when the explorers reached the beautiful city founded by Alexander the Great. They saw the enormous luminous signal light in its entire splendor on the island of Pharos,[87] commemorated by the power of the old Empire of *Hellenistic Greece*.[88]

They flew along the route of the enormous channel of the Nile until they reached the Rashid tributary,[89] and from there they continued south, where they found a spectacle that still impresses the most calloused of travelers: The Pyramids of Gizeh. The suffocating heat of the desert forced them to look a little further south for a refuge. There, they found an oasis near the city of Memphis, capital of Egypt during those times,[90] where they admired the alabaster sphinx, four meters high by

[87] The lighthouse of Alexandria. A tower 120 meters tall, located on the Island of Pharos, built by Ptolemy Philadelphus in 285 B.C. falling to its destruction in 1302 A.C. (Doctors note).

[88] Alexander the Great, King of Macedonia, was made Hellenistic Emperor of the Greeks in Corinth. He conquered Greece and defeated the Persians under the reign of Dario III. He left Greek culture in Asia and Africa as a legacy. At his death (323 B.C.), his empire was divided between his generals, giving rise to the Ptolemaic Dynasty up till the time of Cleopatra. (Doctors note).

[89] Dumyat is another important river's tributary, in Eastern Egypt. (Doctors note).

[90] Precursor of the city of Al Fustat, founded by the Arabs. Now Cairo capital of Egypt. (Doctors note).

alabaster sphinx, four meters high by eight in length, built in honor of the Ptah God[91] in the era of Amenophis II Pharaoh of the XVIII dynasty. There, in that place of paradise, they found a great variety of trees such as sycamores, fig and date, mixed with cypresses, acacias and eucalyptuses. There were large and beautiful Rose bushes and Lotus flowers covering the grounds of the miraculous Eden. The thick forest that made up the small place was a result of the infinite kindness of God. It offered the adventurers a perfect place to take refuge. As if they were exalted sultans, they settled into the hiding place to wait for the night, when they would inspect the Sphinx. After the Astral King hid itself behind the desert horizon of the Sahara, Califax and Hayex went searching for an encounter with the Guardian of Ra.

Under the protection of a moonless night, the valiant explorers began to examine the majestic statue: 20 meters high by 30 meters wide and 65 meters long.[92] Between claws' Sphinx they found, partially covered by sand, a temple built by the Romans in Julius Caesar's day.

They began to dig, expecting to find some kind of conduit that would lead them to the interior of the Sphinx. After a while, they encountered a pair of great doors made of shining brilliant bronze that had been for thousands of in the sands of the desert.

The dragon and the gargoyle tried to open the doors, but their efforts were futile. The door was locked with an almost invisible, strange kind of apparatus at-

---

[91] Apis, the sacred bull. Built around 1580 B.C. (Doctors note).
[92] Diverse sources indicate a variety of dimensions, which range from 39 to 73 meters long. (Doctors note).

tached to the door. However, after inspecting it for several minutes, they discovered a small hole in the bolt. Califax then took his shining sword and introduced the end of the weapon into that small hole. A shining light illuminated the pale face of the Sphinx and as if by magic, the doors opened. To their surprise, they found a steep set of stairs that seemed to lead to some kind of underground chamber. They walked down cautiously and found a wide hallway divided by a large wall. The deep darkness that reigned in that mysterious enclosure reminded them of their experience in the horrifying kingdom of Lugh.

"Not again, please!" Hayex exclaimed in fear. However, Califax, kept his calm, lit a flame with his nose and went into that maze of passages and walls.

After several minutes of walking in the intricate chambers laced with dead ends, they returned to the place from which they had begun.

"This place seems to be as difficult to decipher as the labyrinth of Lugh," observed the dragon.

They started out again, and after a few hours of walking in that stone puzzle, they found a narrow spiral staircase on the other end of the labyrinth. They descended very carefully, but suddenly they fell down a polished surface that made it impossible to return to the first level. That is when they discovered that they were trapped inside the Sphinx. They had no other choice but to keep walking ahead.

Califax lit a flame with his nose again; they found another staircase that seemed to beckon to them. They descended very carefully. They came to a wall that stretched from side to side in front of them; this new chamber had hallways much narrower than the others. They went to the left, and after a short time, they hit an insurmountable wall that forced them to go back from whence they had come. So they returned to where they had started and went to the right this time, the passage led to a long corridor. They did not know it at the time, but they were on the verge of going into an intricate place where only priests and a privileged few knew the way out.

They spent long hours in that labyrinth without finding an exit. The sun illuminated the desert sky, for quite some time, but the adventurers were still trapped by perpetual darkness that prevailed in that eerie site. Desperation encouraged by disorientation and the terrible cold of the chamber that chilled their bodies, undermined the confidence of the explorers. Thirst and hunger joined in. They had not eaten anything for hours, and they had not drunk so much as a drop of water.

"Oh, how I would love to eat a piece of lamb like the one in Athens!" remembered Hayex nostalgically.

"Do not torment your self. We will take a break before going any further. We will get out of here very soon," encouraged Califax with a pat on his shoulder.

"We should be more cautious and bring some food and water, don't you think so, my friend?" asked Hayex, with apprehension.

"Now is not the time to bewail for what we did not do. We should stay calm and we will get out of here alive. If we could get out of the Labyrinth of Lugh, we can get out of this one," Califax encouraged.

𝒯he 𝒮phinx 𝓛abyrinth
𝒻irst level

With renewed sprit, they started out again, and at night-fall, they finally found a long corridor that led to a great chamber, whose walls and columns were exquisitely adorned with large multicolored paintings. At the end of the temple, there was a fabulous bird whose enormous eye hypnotized the explorers. On the bird's head, there was a strange disc, in bas-relief, supported by a stylized *U* that was finished off exotically.[93]

---

[93] A man with hawk's head represented the God Ra, creator and councilor of the Universe, which principal symbol was a solar disc. (Doctors note).

The Sphinx Labyrinth
Second level

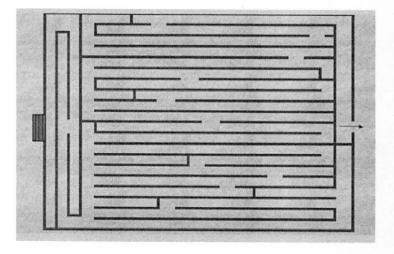

"Have you noticed a strange similarity between human nations?" observed Califax.

"Yes," agreed Hayex. "This eye is similar to the Lugh,[94] not to mention the labyrinth. I would say that, this disc represents the sun," Hayex offered.

"These strange inscriptions must show the way to the Rock of Ebony, that the Magician spoke of; but how are we going to interpret them?" wondered Califax.

Time marched on, inexorably, as they admired and examined the magnificent frescos with curiosity. However, the strange hieroglyphics were incomprehensi-

---

[94] Horus' eye. God of the Sky, the Light, and Goodness. Son of Isis and Osiris and Seth's brother. His eyes represented the sun and the moon. (Doctors note)

ble to the brave explorers who, without giving up, devised the next best thing to make a copy of hieroglyphics. With a copy in their claws, they could seek the help of an interpreter. That debilitating work would be interrupted by an event that hung, as if it were the sword of Damocles, over the unsuspecting amateur archaeologists: The earth announced a tragedy in which they would be buried within a few moments.

"What was that?" Hayex asked alarmed.

"It must have been just a little tremor, my friend," explained Califax.

"While we are in here, no tremor seems little to me," retorted Hayex with stark fear in his voice.

Suddenly, the place was shaking furiously and the sand began to filter between the rocks, the ceiling and the walls of the chamber. Terrified by that violent movement, Califax and Hayex felt their time had come. Everything indicated that the Great Sphinx would devour them. It seemed that their last resting place was going to be inside the underground temple and, consequently, cause them to fail in their mission.

Califax could not hold the flame in his nose any longer, and the deep darkness of the place seized the very soul of the adventurers. However, Hayex, who had squirmed into a corner of one of the walls, pushed the door of a cavity that seemed to lead to a secret passage, which they had not noticed before.

The gargoyle quickly advised his companion about his fortunate discovery, and they hastily left the chamber. Seconds later it collapsed, totally, with a great crash.

The dragon ignited a flame with his nose and the light revealed three small, but steep, sloping hallways leading upwards at a sharp angle. Because of his large size, Califax had to drag himself up in order to travel along that small suffocating crawl space, while Hayex followed close behind. They took the hallway to the right. They advanced very slowly until they arrived to a very damp place that seemed like a gallery, where they took a breather.

"What a strange place!" said the dragon as he lit the upper portion and ceiling of the chamber.

Califax took one step forward, while he meticulously examined the place he unexpectedly disappeared from Hayex's site, and the gallery turned completely dark.

"Califax! Califax!" shouted the terrified gargoyle from the edge of the gallery.

When he did not get an answer, he groped his way over to the place where Califax had disappeared. He found a deep hole, where his faithful companion had surly fallen.

The gargoyle agonized over the loss his friend. Suddenly, he heard Califax's voice. He hung precariously on a rock that was sticking out of one of the walls of the deep hole, just on the other side of where the dragon had fallen. Unfortunately, the hole was not wide enough for him to flap his powerful wings, so he held tight to his support made of rock, lit his nose and analyzed his predicament. Hayex then saw the grave situation his friend was in and without thinking twice, headed down to try to help him. Hayex pushed on the tail of the heavy reptile, but he had no luck in moving him even one inch.

Califax soon began to loose strength and he was in danger of falling to the bottom of the stinking flooded pit. Seconds later, the inevitable happened: Califax let go of the rock and fell heavily, dragging the poor unfortunate gargoyle along with him.

Interior of the Sphinx

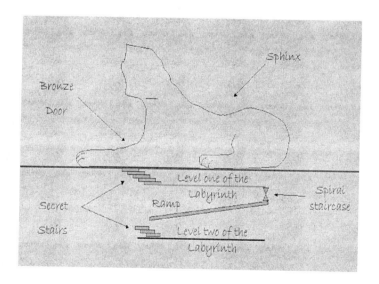

Fortunately, the hole was not as deep as it looked, the reflective water had kept them from seeing the bottom, but Califax could not help but fall on top of his friend, who, once again, was covered with dirty, sticky mud.

"Again?" protested the gargoyle, angrily as he shook the mud from his body.

"Perhaps your true vocation is pottery, my friend," said Califax, making light of the situation.

After that bitter experience, they saw a series of rocks protruding from the walls of the hole that formed a sort of stairway, which allowed them to climb up and to continue walking along the hallway from which Califax had fallen. The tunnel extended for several meters until reaching a vertex that lead them into a new chamber, where they found many beautiful objects made of ceramic, wood and pure gold, but the walls were bare, contrasting starkly from the beautiful walls of the Sphinx temple.

Again, they began to examine the chamber to see if they could find a way out. While they were doing this, Hayex tripped on an enormous object that, when he saw what it was, left him breathless. What he was looking at was nothing less than, the sarcophagus of Cheops, mummy and all. They had penetrated the chamber of the King of the Great Pyramid.

Hours passed as they searched for an exit from the tomb. Hayex had already lost hope of ever escaping their ill-fated trap.

"Solomon told us that no one had ever lived to tell the story of leaving this place, my friend," pronounced a frightened Hayex.

"Keep calm, my friend. I am sure that there is a way out. Listen!" he indicated with ears perked sharply.

A soft sound indicated that an air current ran through the place. Thanks to his excellent hearing, Califax managed to find the source of the air current. High in one of the walls, they found a hole that seemed to be some kind of air duct. They saw a dim light coming through from the other side of the cavity. Then Califax took his magic sword and put the end of it in the hole, after which, a flood of fine sand filled the room, threatening to bury the explorers alive. However, the sandy flood stopped when it reached the halfway mark of the chamber.

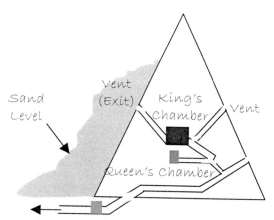

Cheops Pyramid
(Interior Diagram)

When the vent was emptied, the vesper light of the sun shown through for the first time in centuries on the King's chamber, revealing its valuable treasures; but, for the travelers, it was the invaluable road to freedom.

They exited on the west side of the pyramid and observed in astonishment, that the desert sand had covered the illustrious Sphinx to its neck. The tremendous earthquake that had so furiously shook them made the Sphinx fall heavily on top of the two levels that supported it, burying the terrible prophecies and the valuable treasures forever.

The Sphinx after the Earthquake

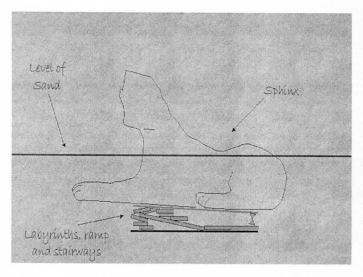

"Now, how are we going to find the man to whom we must deliver the Chalice?" Califax asked, afflicted, to the gargoyle

The afternoon languished in the desert steppe along with the hopes of the daring adventurers. Everything indicated that, the important mission that the dragon had been assigned, had become a complete failure.

The Secret of the Dragon

8

The Rock of Kaabah

CALIFAX AND HAYEX TOOK REFUGE IN THE OASIS OF Memphis, while the night overpowered the desert in an unusual halo of tranquility. The dragon saw his mother in a dream at the foot of the Sphinx, guided by the claw of his handsome father, who pointed his sword in the same direction as the enigmatic statue's stare.

Califax woke up from his strange dream with a start, and immediately woke his tired, sleeping friend.

"Hayex! Hayex!" he shouted with enthusiasm

"What happened?" said a groggy Hayex.

"I have it!" shouted Califax.

"What do you have?" he asked doubtful gargoyle.

"I know where the Rock of Ebony is!" announced a jubilant Califax.

"Really…? Where?"

"The Magician, said: *The guardian of Ra, the sun of the east, indicates the secret way to the Rock of Ebony,*" he remembered. "The Sphinx *shows* the way, it does not hold the secret within. Do you understand?"

"No," he answered with a disinterested yawn.

"The Sphinx looks to the east," insisted the dragon. "That is where the Rock must be!"

"Do you really think so?" said the gargoyle doubtfully.

At dawn, the dragon and the gargoyle traveled southeast crossing the vast desert, and later crossed the Gulf of Suez and of the Aqaba. They were almost to the Sinai Peninsula. From there, they could see the 2,637 meter high Biblical Mountain, where Moses was given the Sacred Law of God which up to our time, has fallen on the deaf ears and hardened hearts of men and nations of this world.

After crossing the Red Sea, they came the Hejaz Mountains, to the west of the Al-Arab[95] Peninsula, where they saw a caravan of merchants traveling south.

Without knowing where to look for the Rock of Ebony, they decided to join that procession, hidden under their customary disguises: their objective was to interrogate some of the nomads. Discreetly, they joined that long line of people, horses and camels that carried all kinds of merchandise from all over the world. When they saw that Califax was not carrying anything, a merchant placed a large bundle of objects and heavy bags on his back.

---

[95] Arabia. In Arabic, it means *Island of Arabs*. (Doctors note).

"Here, in the desert, even royalty has to help with the caravan," he said, as he violently placed the heavy items on the dragon's back.

Hearing the merchant speak Gaelic, Hayex took advantage of the situation and approached him asking:

"Excuse me, Sir, but do you know where can I find the Rock of Ebony?"

"No such thing exists, son. Ebony is a type of wood, which is indeed, is black and hard," he said, without even giving the gargoyle a second glance.

"What I am looking for is a Sacred Rock. Someone told me that it is called the Rock of Ebony, Sir," he insisted, after discreetly glancing at the dragon.

"I told you that thing does not exist!" he shouted in the gargoyle's face. "However," he said, this time a little more friendly, "the Sacred Rock of Kaabah is black. Maybe, your informant is referring to that Rock, my friend."

"Do you know where it is located?" Hayex asked.

"Of course. It is in the City of Macoraba,[96] we are going that way."

Following the caravan through the desert, the daring travelers arrived at Port al-Wajh, where the merchants took a break while they offered their rich display of merchandise for sale to the population of the city.

After spending the night in al-Wajh, they continued south following the *"uadi"*[97] el-Hamd Rivera. The long crossing under an intense heat of the sun, had begun to undermine Califax's strength and his feet and back

[96] Ancient name for Mecca or Makkah. (Doctors note).
[97] Arab word meaning *riverbed*. (Doctors note).

began to ache under the immense weight of his load. However, the dragon continued along walking without mentioning the heavy mass or complaining.

The Arab Caravan

Six days and five nights went by before they reached the City of Yathrib,[98] where the caravan finally stopped. However a few days prior to their arrival, an imposing sand storm had wrapped around them with its ominous reddish mantle, forcing them to walk even slower. The furious attack of the sand storm on the caravan was so violent that they finally had to stop to protect themselves

---

[98] Later called, Medina or al-Madinah Rasul Allah, *City of the Prophet of God.* (Doctors note).

from being buried under the hot embrace of the desert. After the storm blew over, the leaders decided to have a little healthy fun for the men. They organized a traditional camel race, where the winner would take a wineskin full of red wine as the grand prize. For obvious reasons, Califax and Hayex were not interested in competing in the event, but their refusal was negated, 'in a friendly manner' by a group of ill-tempered Koreish men[99]

The competitors prepared their camels and took their positions. Hayex put a scarlet turban on his head and covered his face according to the custom of the nomads and mounted the back of Califax as an experienced Jockey. The route of the race was drawn around the campground, and they would run counterclockwise. Whoever ran the first nine stipulated laps, would be the winner of the wineskin.

"Are you ready, my friend?" the gargoyle asked nervously.

"Perhaps. You are not even thinking that we are in this competition to win?" surprised, asked the dragon.

"Well. A wineskin would do us no harm," teased Hayex.

"I am not a camel! Don't you realize that I cannot compete against them?" Califax complained.

"Of course, you can! On the Island of Cyprus you ran as fast as you fly, my friend," he reminded him.

The judge of the race gave the starting signal with a huge flag. The gallop of the noble brutes kicked up the sand as if they were a big storm. The spectators were

---

[99] Arabic tribe made up of ten of the most important clans. (Doctors note).

moved to shout with emotion, they cheered their favorites on while they waved their sharp and brilliant scimitars.[100]

After three quick rounds, Califax and Hayex came close to the lead, but they found themselves behind three camels, which blocked their passage in an aggressive manner, pushing them violently to the center. Then, Califax took the inside curve to avoid crashing into the ignoble competitors. It caused him to skid and he almost fell on his inexpert rider. However, he kept his four paws on the burning sand and continued in the race.

In the seventh lap, the reckless runners continued looking for a chance to pass their fierce opponents, who at the same time were doing everything within their power to prevent such a move.

In the ninth and final lap, every thing that they had tried had failed, and the race had turned into a personal issue with those select Arabs. Weary of their cheating stratagems, Califax decided to fight fire with *fire*. Close to the finish line, the nomads formed a roadblock in front of the dragon, but just a few meters from the end of the race, a blaze on the buttocks of the mounts. The frightened camels reared and crashed against each other until they finally came to a screeching halt and flung their Arab riders headlong into the burning sand. While the cheating Arabs were lying in the sand, our intrepid sportsmen crossed the finish line with ease.

The entire caravan applauded them; they were taken to the center of the camp where they were awarded. Nobody noticed the trick they had used to win the race,

---

[100] A curved blade from western Asia. (Doctors note).

because the flame the dragon sent out was hidden by the enormous amount of dust that their opponents kicked up.

Califax was awarded a basket full of sweet fruit and a huge water container, while Hayex was carried on the shoulders of the men as he leisurely drank from the large wineskin. Everyone wanted to see the winner's faces, but as could be expected, the adventurers refused such a request. However, there is little discussion with an Arab who has made up his mind.

The Arabs jumped on top of them and took off their disguises. When they saw their to them, horrid faces, they poised themselves in a battle stance, attacked with their scimitars in front of them, and invoked the sacred name of Allah.

Hayex flew, quickly, away to avoid being hurt by the sharp weapons, but Califax was defenseless because his wings were tied to his back, there was nothing to do to save himself in the middle of that irascible crowd.

The rabble hesitated, having fallen prey to fear, which gave the dragon time to free his tail and wings. He unfolded them before the would-be killers, changed his scales to an intense reddish brown color, sat up on his hind legs and released a great flame to the sky, accompanied by blood-curdling roar that stopped the enemy in their tracks. The people of the caravan then took a step back from the magnificent beast, and Califax took advantage of the moment to pick up his clothes and retreat from the area.

After the men came to their senses, they insulted the brave globetrotters brandishing their weapons with a new and unknown epithet: *"Pazuzu! Pazuzu!"*[101]

"Perhaps we should follow the caravan from on high in the mountains," suggested the dragon.

"I told you we could win the race, my friend!" said Hayex, with glee. "Many times, the worst enemy can be our own doubts, my friend," concluded the gargoyle as he continued drank happily from the wineskin.

Hidden behind the arid mountains, the travelers followed the caravan to the City of Yathrib, where they tried to find food so that they could continue their dangerous mission.

Under the protection of the night, Hayex took care of the task of supplying them with food, hiding himself under the legs of the camels. He found a good amount of fruit, dried meat and water sacks packed on the backs of two or three camels. So as not to be noticed, he placed the supplies on the back of the dragon, as if he was just another merchant with his camel, and they left the City of Yathrib to hide in the crook of the river. Since the time they had adventured into the entrails of the Sphinx, their meals had been few. They agreed to have a goodly feast before falling deep into blissful sleep until the next morning.

The day broke with the suffocating sun of the East, and the daring adventurers got ready to continue their exciting mission. They got up very early to watch

---

[101] An ancient demon of Mesopotamia as God of the wind and desert storm, he was represented by a human figure with a tail, four wings on his back and spurs on his hands and feet. (Doctors note).

from on high as the caravan prepared. Following the Hejaz Mountains, the caravan took a southeasterly route. Twelve days went by before the caravan completed the 400-kilometer trip that separated Yathrib from Macoraba,[102] but this time the trip had been more benign other than the heat as they crossed the tropic of Cancer.

The magnificent City of Macoraba was full of faithful pilgrims waiting to pay tribute and to cleanse their sins before the sacred icon in the hermitage of Kaabah. Califax and Hayex observed and studied the movements of the visitors from a prudent distance. They had to wait for an opportune moment before venturing inside the temple. After several hours, afternoon approached and the crowd seemed to grow larger. The dragon and gargoyle grew impatient as they watched.

The devoted pilgrims came from Greece, the Desert of Nubia[103] and even as far as Nineveh,[104] to have their prayers heard. They deposited statuettes around the sanctuary, in which, many pilgrims, entered for a short time. The sanctuary was formed in the shape of a cube and was made up of grey rock and black marble, supported by three huge columns inside.

"Do you think is the Rock of Ebony that we are looking for?" asked the gargoyle.

"It is too big. I think the rock we are looking for is inside. Look how the men go in and out of it!" observed the dragon.

"Then we will have to go in," stated Hayex.

---

[102] Ancestral name of Mecca. Named this way by Ptolemy in the II century B.C. (Doctors note).
[103] Sudan, in Eastern Africa. (Doctors note).
[104] Now the City of Al-Mawsil (Mosul) in northern Iraq. (Doctors note).

"It would be better to wait until evening, don't you think?" suggested Califax.

The Mosque of Kaabah

The stars were opaque against the crescent moon rising in the east, when Califax and Hayex donned their usual disguises and ventured into the sanctuary of Kaabah. The place was empty, and a strange silence prevailed. Side-stepping the enormous number of small statuettes that the pilgrims had placed around the temple, the infidels silently penetrated the tabernacle.

The great number of paintings and engravings of diverse Mediterranean gods, that adorned the place,[105] marveled the tireless globetrotters. In the eastern corner of the temple, they found a strange black rock surrounded by a stone ring.[106]

"Great! It seems that we have found the Rock of Ebony. And so, now what?" asked Hayex, halfheartedly.

"I do not know. Perhaps we will find something here that will guide us to our destiny," said the dragon.

Tray as they might, they could not find anything that showed them the way to complete their mission. After a thorough examination of the place, they accepted the fact that what they sought was not to be found at the Temple of Kaabah. They walked over to a nearby spring and drank from its waters. They were oblivious to the fact that they were being watched by a small group of men who relentlessly guarded the sanctuary day and night. While eagerly drinking from the clear and refreshing waters, the men surprised them wielding enormous scimitars. Startled, they quickly took off their disguises and flew away without even knowing the reason for this latest aggression. "Blasphemy! They have profaned the sacred Zamzam![107]" they heard the men shout, while they flew away protected by the dark mantle of night. Once again, the shadow of failure showed its face to the adventures.

[105] When Muhammad took Mecca, in 630 A.C., he commanded the pagan paintings and statuettes of Kaabah to be destroyed. (Doctors note).
[106] A white rock was given to Adam after his expulsion from Eden, which was reconstructed by Abraham and Ishmael. According to legend, the rock turned black after absorbing the sins of thousands of pilgrims that came to touch it throughout the centuries. (Doctors note).
[107] Legend states that Hagar, Abraham's second wife, mother of Ishmael, drank water from this sacred spring. (Doctors note).

"This is the end of the mission, my friend. I do not think we can find the man we are looking for," said the dragon with a heavy heart.

Meanwhile, in Dragonia, the situation was not any better. The incessant attacks of the Selenex caused countless causalities on both sides. All the while, empty speeches resonated all over the *Region of Fire*.

An important meeting between the two kings and tribes had taken place in Amerux, official seat of the League of Dragons. Their objective was to make a peace treaty. Palux, King of the Selenex, confirmed his intention for peace and harmony with the Helenex. In an emotional speech before the high dignitaries, Palux proclaimed,

"...And I will always carry, in my right claw, this olive branch as a symbol of peace, and in the right, an arrow to defend it, even at the cost of my own life."

The rabid applause resonated in the enormous enclosure, indicating the popular approval of the peace agreement. However, the incipient truce could not be held for long because of differences that existed between the tribes. The Amerux, allies of the Helenex, accused the Arbux tribe of hiding their activities from the League of Dragons and blatantly supporting the Selenex by providing military training, arms and a safe refuge for Dragonia aggressors. The Arbux categorically denied the accusations illicit practices. However, the Amerux Intelligence Agency had information that supported the accusations. Although, most of the tribes condemned an attack on the Arbux, the last word would come from the jaws of the Amerux, the most powerful tribe in the *Region of Fire*.

Thus, the dragons tried to clarify their differences. Beyond that of the ominous prophecies of the Sacred Papyruses that warned the *Region of Fire*, wrapped them in their ignorance, they would be incinerated in a bonfire lit by lies and hate, suspicion and intolerance, as well as in that of the dark hidden agendas of those in power that, inevitably, would lead to the extinction of these irrational beasts.

The rising sun shined over the Eastern steppe of the Arabian Peninsula, and the brave globetrotters could not shake the misery and frustration brought on by their failed attempt to complete the mission. However, arming themselves with courage and patience, they decided not to waver in their endeavor. They wandered in the desert, unsuccessfully, for several days trying to find the man who would activate the power of the Chalice. They looked in every oasis, cave and shrub, hoping to find a sign that would indicate the way; but they found nothing.

They moved, persistently, forward. They had long since overcome their fear of men. They joined yet another caravan of merchants who were traveling north where they hope to obtain some information from a nomad, but the days passed without the possibility of achieving their goal.

One night, Hayex sat close to an old man near the heat of a bonfire, in spite of his blindness, he seemed to see life with a great deal of clarity. After some small talk, the man began to speak profoundly to the gargoyle.

"What is it that you are looking for in this desert Hayex?" he asked in a friendly manner.

"I am looking for a very special man," he answered dejectedly.

Map of Europe

7th Century

"What is so special about that man for whom you look for?" asked the old man.

"I really do not know," answered Hayex, honestly.

"If you dig deep in their heart, you will find that all men are special," stated the old man.

"All men are the same to me, Sir," Hayex objected, remembering only the horrors of men.

"Many centuries ago, a fisherman proclaimed that all men are as special as every fish in his net."

"All fish are the same, Sir," he said, impatiently.

"There was once a pilgrimage where a large crowd of people gathered to listen to the words of that fisherman," continued the old man. "They were together for three days and they were hungry. Then, from one basket with seven pieces of bread and a few fish, he fed a multitude that surpassed five thousand people," he related.

"But... That is impossible!" exclaimed the gargoyle in disbelief.

"Who knows? Nevertheless, for each one of those people, the fish that they ate was particularly special since it satisfied their hunger."

"I realize what you are saying, Sir, but I do not think you understand what I am trying to say," he explained. "This man has something *very special* that I need."

"A person becomes special because of what we offer them, not because of what we receive from them. You have to keep in mind that you must sow before you reap. Only then will you find what you are looking for," concluded the old man.

The light of a half moon illuminated the serene desert steppe and the traveler fell prey to the fatigue of the day, sleeping peacefully until dawn, safe and secure within the caravan.

The next day was no more fruitful than the last, even in spite of their laborious and relentless investigation among the Arabs in the long caravan; the adventurers were not able to find any useful information to help them reach their objective. They decided to leave the caravan to look for their objective in other desert areas, but they had to do this at an opportune time so as not to raise suspicion among the humans.

The moment came before they expected it. Just before dusk, a whirling sand storm began besieged the caravan. The column of merchants was prepared for the storm, taking shelter and waiting patiently for the thrashing wind to pass. The profound darkness of the torrid wind provided our valiant adventurers a perfect cover to escape furtively from the inquisitive eyes of the nomads.

Fighting against the powerful force of the winds, they flew towards the Hejaz Mountain slopes, where they hoped the strength of the storm would diminish. After a short time, the storm finally died down and the brave travelers discussed the course that they would follow next.

"It would be better to go north. I do not think we will find the man we are looking for here," suggested the gargoyle.

"Perhaps, but remember that the Magician spoke about the Rock of Ebony. I think that it must be very close," encouraged the dragon.

"If we are mistaken about the rock, Califax?" asked Hayex.

"The Sphinx directed us to this place. Besides, I do not think there are many rocks like the one in Macoraba," reasoned Califax.

"I seem to remember seeing some caves not very far from here. Perhaps we can find some clues there. I will take a look while you rest a bit," offered the gargoyle. "You have carried a heavy load for a very long time now, my friend, so it is my turn," smiled the gargoyle.

Hayex quickly flew away and his small figure disappeared in the immensity of the brilliant desert sun. Meanwhile Califax got his enormous body comfortable in the shade of a gigantic cedar and drank from the water bags that the gargoyle had stolen from the Arabs. Within only a few minutes, the dragon fell into a deep and refreshing sleep.

Califax was deep within a dark cave. The intense cold of the cave contrasted with the extreme heat of the desert that he had taken refuge from. Then, from the deepest part of the grotto, he heard a sonorous voice ask him: *"Would you drink of my blood, Califax?"* as the macabre voice spat out a ridiculing laughter.

The sun fell, announcing dusk, when Califax awakened with a start. Time had flown and Hayex had still not returned. Anxiousness made him look in the nearby areas for his astute companion, but he could not find him. The dragon reproached himself for having left his faithful comrade alone for yet a second time.

Nighttime surprised Califax while he searched exhaustively for his companion. He searched every tree and crevice without finding him. He even looked under rocks, but it seemed that the desert had simply swallowed Hayex. Just thinking about it gave Califax an intense chill that traveled all the way to the bones of his body. He anxiously scoured the countryside in search of his friend. Shouted his name and he send huge flames in the air so that the gargoyle could locate him. The only answer he got, was from the ululate wind.

After several hours of intensive searching, Califax's sensitive ears heard some loud guffaws not too far away. He stealthily approached the place were he heard the voices and finally found his comrade. If he was not in the best of situations, at least he was still alive.

Hayex had been taken prisoner and he was being held inside a wooden cage, guarded by two nasty looking men who talked while they eagerly ate lamb, roasting on the fire.

"What do you think?" asked one of the men. "Perhaps we can exhibit it in a circus. Even Cesar himself would pay a fortune to see this animal!" the villain exclaimed.

"What do you think it is? I have never seen such a horrible creature," said the other, scoundrel as he stared into the gargoyles terrified eyes.

Hidden behind the trees, Califax watched the movements of the nomads very carefully. They appeared to be caravan thieves and robbers. In spite of his size, the dragon had to be very careful while rescuing his friend, since a thief, feared nothing when it came to defending their ill-gotten booty.

"If it dies of hunger? We do not know what this thing eats," observed one of the kidnapers.

"If it dies, we can eat it. I do not think that its meat would be so bad. Later, we could sell or exhibit his skeleton in some circus," said the other thief, violently tearing the flesh from the lamb leg. Hayex was paralyzed with fear. He drowned out a scream of terror when he read the wicked expressions on the faces of the thieves.

Califax waited patiently for sleep to overcome the scoundrels, before rescuing the gargoyle. Once they were asleep, the dragon stealthily approached the cage where Hayex lay awake in fear. Signaling silence to the gargoyle with his index claw, the dragon stealthily approached the cage. His carefully laid plans to save his friend were thwarted by the whinny of the horses. The whinnying aroused the bandits.

"We are being robbed!" complained one of the unscrupulous thieves.

The nomads quickly jumped to their feet and unsheathed their scimitars. They were pointed in the direction of their aggressor hiding in the shadows of the night. Then Califax jumped between the men and the caged Hayex. Standing on his hind legs, he opened his huge wings to intimidate and scare away the kidnappers. Not these thieves. Their greed outweighed their fear and they wanted nothing more than to ensnare the young dragon.

"We have to capture him alive! This will surly make us rich!"

Califax, became very angry and changed his color to an intense red while drawing his brilliant sword and opening fire on the evildoers, who covered themselves like magic with Roman shields, items that were surly stolen in some robbery.

The thieves attacked their fabulous enemy brandishing their sabers and shouting dreadful war cries. With just one strike of his sword, Califax split the scimitars of his attackers in half. When they realized that they had been disarmed, they ran toward their horses that had long since fled the scene.

After Hayex had been freed from his prison, the daring adventurers flew to the infertile hills of Arabia under the protection afforded them by the dark night.

After find a safe refuge, they lit a bonfire and they ate some fruit, and dried meat.

"How did they capture you?" asked Califax, intrigued.

"I do not know. They surprised me with a net while I was coming out of a cave. I do not understand how I did not see them before."

"Forget it, my friend. You are safe now," Califax reassured his friend.

A long silence overcame the jaws of the explorers, but after a time, Califax spoke.

"I never asked you about your family, Hayex. Tell me about them," he asked.

"A long time ago, I lost them at the hands of men, my friend," he remembered with great sorrow. "My parents and grandparents, together with eight of my brothers and sisters, lived very happily in the southern forest of the Island of Briton, along with many other gargoyles. One day, two of our kind went exploring in a human village where they were captured. The humans killed them in a very cruel manner, covered them with clay and baked their cadavers. They later placed them in the mouth of several water drainages at the top of a bell tower as a warning to the '*Dark Demons of Averno,*' as they called us, to stay away from their houses."

"And you and your people did not keep to a safe distance from them?" asked a horrified the dragon.

"After that tragedy, nobody dared approach that place again. However, the humans thought that there must be more of us and they came looking. They started a huge forest fire that surprised us while we were sleeping and then they attacked with rocks and arrows. After the attack, we went north, but the humans spread the word, warning the rest of the humans of our existence. Although, there was a great slaughter in the last siege, I managed to escape, but I did not return to see about my family. The hunt lasted for years, until we were practically extinct. I wandered the island for a long time in hopes of finding more of my kind, but alas, I only found them mounted as water drainages on top of many different houses. Then I met you, my friend. I think I am the last of my kind," Hayex whispered.

After he heard Hayex's sad story, Califax fell silent. He contemplated his blessings and he felt a little guilty for having a home, a nice family and very good friends in Dragonia. In spite of an overwhelming sense of sorrow for Hayex's plight, he thought about the many beings who carry burdens and suffering in their heart each day. Being one of the privileged few, he had many things to be thankful to his god, Helion.

"You are no longer alone, my dear friend. When this adventure is over, we will look for your kin. Surely, your kin are equally as astute as you are. Surely many of your kind managed to escape the wrath of men," the dragon encouraged in order cheering his comrade.

The shadows stretched out as the moon fell on the horizon, and the audacious adventurers buried their sadness in the reassuring arms of Morpheus.

The Secret of the Dragon

.

9

The Prophet of the Cave

THE DESERT STEPPE GLOW IN GOLDEN SPLENDOR, AS the dragon and the gargoyle prepared themselves to continue their mission after a large breakfast of fruit and dried meat. Their diet had not changed for quite some time. Surprisingly enough they began to miss the taste of fish. After hiding their food and clothes behind some scrubs, they took flight. Even having found an excellent hiding place, Califax kept the bag containing the valuable cup with him at all times.

They flew all around Macoraba looking for anything that might lead them to the mysterious man who would activate the Chalice. The only thing they found was the discomfort from the cruel and implacable heat of the desert.

When the vigorous sun god reached its zenith, a powerful storm surprised the valiant globetrotters. So intensely did they search that they failed to notice the approaching storm. It was impossible for them to escape the storm by flight. The dragon and the gargoyle fought to keep sight of each other as the headed for refuge behind some large rocks. When the storm passed, the landscape had changed drastically. The large amount of wind blown sand covered the original geography, causing the expeditionary to become lost. Their anguish and frustration increased when they discovered that the relentless power of the desert had yanked their water supply from them. Only one wineskin remained, with just a few sips of the vital liquid.

They flew for several hours searching for their hiding place, or an oasis from which to replenish their water supply. Their search was fruitless. The dunes filled the countryside, as far as the eye could see, spreading in a perpetual sea of sand and loneliness.

A few hours after midday, the luminosity of the desert began to strangely change its tone, as if a huge cloud were impeding the rays of sunlight. As they looked to the sky an unusual phenomenon appeared before their eyes: The sun seemed to be devoured by the moon. Califax then, remembered the words of the prophecies and the calculations of the astronomers: *"The Earth will be surrounded by darkness in a period of nine months. This is all the time we have..."* It had been almost nine months since had departed from Dragonia, and the mission was not complete. The Helion god was preparing to annihilate the *Region of Fire* and, perhaps, the entire world with a scathing wrath.

The lack of water was taking its toll on the traveler's bodies. Hopelessness was enveloped their spirits. Much too debilitated to fly, they walked in search of some place that will provide them the refreshing alleviation of a shade and a little water.

"Only a sip of water is left. You drink it. You need it in order to finish the mission," said Hayex, on the verge of collapse.

"Thank you, Hayex, but it would be better if you drank it. You need it more than I do, my friend," countered the dragon, almost dieing.

After an exhausting walk on the sand, they reached the foothills of the mountain. While the inexorable passage of the moon covered the sun, the sinister darkness seized the entire region.

Having fallen prey to fear and uncertainty in light of the strange phenomenon, the audacious adventurers looked for a refuge to protect themselves from the imminent attack of Helion's wrath. Debilitated, they climbed to the top of a knoll and found a cave whose mouth was so large that even a regiment of armored dragons could enter it without difficulty. The enormous ceiling of the cave provided comfortable shade that immediately refreshed the overheated comrades.

After recovered their breath, they searched for some water deep into the grotto, but only found the echo of their own steps.

Califax, weak and dehydrated, he could not maintain the fire from his nose for long, and the deep cave quickly surrounded them with its dismal darkness. Totally exhausted and thirsty, they fell into a deep sleep:

prelude of a slumber from which they might never awake.

Outside, the moon continued devouring the sun with its insatiable pace. The darkness became increasingly intense, as did the fear and panic it instilled in the minds of men. They called the cosmic demonstration of godly power, a *bad omen*. The people in the villages and cities ran frantically to their houses, looking for protection for their children and themselves, but found no consolation for their affliction.

Some contemplative and others submissive, the entire population prayed. Even those who previously had denied their belief in prayer, prayed. The prayers of all were for a last-minute forgiveness of all their terrible sins before death overtook them.

Meanwhile, in the cave, Califax woke up after hearing some moaning in the intense darkness. At first, he thought that it was Hayex making those rumbling noises that sounded like a death rattles. Embracing him affectionately, he felt great pain and sadness for his friend's condition. He languished with the blue face of impeding doom.

"I should not have let you come with me," he reproached himself. "I have only brought you here to see you die," he sobbed.

While he held his dear friend in his claws, Califax heard the moaning again and noticed that they did not come from the gargoyle, but rather from somewhere deeper in the cave. Then, Hayex miraculously awoke.

"What is going on, my friend? Why are you crying?" he asked, coming out of his lethargy.

"Shhh! There is someone else here," Califax said, pointing deeper into the cave.

Silently they approached the source of the moaning, only to find a man who seemed to be dieing. With his clothes torn and his face badly burnt by the sun, the man lay on his back, speaking incoherent words seemingly torn from some horrible nightmare; he appeared to have been beaten by the implacable power of the Arabic Desert. Taking pity on the unfortunate man, Califax took the last of the water and pored it in the Chalice, while Hayex watched in ceremonious silence as he observed the unselfish act.

The dragon gave the man two or three sips, and he suddenly regained consciousness. Califax immediately put out the fire from his nose so as not to be seen by the man. Meanwhile, outside, an enormous and beautiful solar crown was revealed behind the dark disc of the moon, submerging the entire region in the unusual darkness that afternoon before the arrival of summer.

Inside of the cave, the eternal darkness surrounded that strange meeting of beings, all from a very different nature and culture. Suddenly, an intense white light illuminated the whole place. Quickly, the dragon and the gargoyle left the man's side and pressed their backs against the cold wall of the cave. The intense light that seemed to come from everywhere, and nowhere, seemed to direct itself to the man, who miraculously recovered his strength.

Despite the prodigious manifestation, the daring adventurers felt no fear. They felt that by some miracle, some way, the light had replenished their strength.

Slowly, the light diminished in intensity as it took a strange form, which looked like a man or a dragon, or perhaps both. Without moving from the wall of the cave, the witnesses did not miss a single detail of what was going on in the cavern. Then, that luminous form unfolded two enormous white wings that scattered sparkles all over the grotto when it flapped them.

Still in disbelief, the dragon and the gargoyle felt strangely comforted before the presence of that being, whose powerful, yet soft, voice spoke to the man, and his voice sounded like the oceans song.

"Pray, in the name of Allah, the Beneficent, the Merciful, read in the name of your Lord who created, He created man from a clot. Read and your Lord is most honorable, who taught with the pen, taught man what he knew not."[108]

The man was moved by this and knelt down.

"Hear me, I have been sent here by the Divine Power, to name you the messenger of His Word," he added in a soft and reverent voice.

"Who am I to receive such a high honor, angelical creature? I am but a humble servant of the Highest one on high," said kneeling the man.

"I am the Archangel who holds the Sword of Fire.[109] I am the one who advises men of the coming of He who Is, Has Been and Will Be. The time is near, and He will divulge the Sacred Word through your mouth, among the ancestry of Hagar,"[110] he announced.

---

[108] The Sacred Koran 96.1 (Doctors note).

[109] Gabriel (Doctors note).

[110] Abraham's second wife, mother of Ishmael, father of the Arab race. (Doctors note).

"Oh, you that have chained the dark Enemy in his eternal dwelling! You that protect the rock given to us by our father Abraham! If it is the will of the benefactor and the merciful Allah, that I be His messenger, instill eternal knowledge in the mouth of this unfaithful one, and strengthen his feet in order that he may to carry out such a high command," said the man.

"The one who has drunk from His Chalice is worthy of carrying His message. He will be a fisher of men who throws His nets in the desert, as earlier they were thrown," concluded that celestial being.

After that Divine Revelation, the angel disappeared and the cave returned to darkness. Califax and Hayex noticed that thirst and hunger had abandoned them, and before putting the Chalice back inside the sack, the dragon observed a golden light that came from its bottom. The power of that cup, it seemed, had been activated. When leaving the cave, the adventurers noticed with great relief that the world was not destroyed by the wrath of Helion, and that the sun shone with all its usual intensity. Everything looked the same; nevertheless, they had been witness to an event that would change the history course: The anointment of Mohammad, the Prophet of the Cave.

After regaining their strength, the next day the travelers prepared to return to Briton after locating their refuge where they hidden their food and disguises. They needed no more disguises. They left the disguise in that inhospitable place, taking with them only the royal cape. Good spirits had returned to their hearts. They were certain that they had found in that cave the man that they had searched for so long. All that remained was to return to Dragonia to save it from Helion's terrible fire.

They flew in an easterly direction bordering the coast of the Red Sea until reaching the River Nile. From there, they went to the Island of Crete, and later they reached the tip of the Italian boot after hours of fatiguing flight over the Ionian Sea.

Once again, they managed to crosses the Italian Pennine Alps and the treacherous French Alps. After two days, the gargoyle felt at home again when reaching Calais.

"Finally, Briton!" exclaimed Hayex with a sigh. "Now that the power of the Chalice has been activated, what are you going to do with it?" he asked to the dragon.

"I must give it to Filox. Surely, he will know what to do," He said with conviction.

They ate a large amount of fish and took a short rest before starting out again on their trip home. They felt a great sense of satisfaction in having succeeded in ac-complishing their mission.

It was midday before the successful adventures reached Canterbury. From there, they flew to the city of Londinium to later line up directly towards Stour-in-Usmere.

The golden pastures of Briton were turning green again, and when the night covered them with its dark mantle, the dragon and the gargoyle slept. Califax could not fall asleep. His anxiety over the realization that he was, imminently, going to be home kept him awake. He embraced his prized trophy. It represented a just retribution for his dedication and effort. He curled up among the shrubs and let his heavy eyelids drop down over his tired eyes as he was sung to sleep by the smooth murmur of the dense forest.

The dawn filtered tenuous rays of sunlight through the darkness of the wooded area, and the optimistic travelers continued their trip in high sprits.

Bordering the Snowdon Mountains, they reached the well-known village of Bangor, where the Celts still conserved their traditions and prepared for the traditional '*Beltane*' celebration.[111]

They crossed the Irish Sea until reaching the Isle of Man, where Hayex tried, and failed, again to capture a cat. A little before nightfall, they reached Glasgow, and in the surrounding area they found a safe refuge. All the adventures that they had lived through together in order to obtain the Chalice seemed so far away from the dragon's mind as his thoughts returned to his home.

"We are very close now, my friend. Soon we will be home," encouraged, Califax.

The shadows lengthened and announced the night's arrival. The experienced adventurers got ready to sleep and rest from their exciting journey. Califax as usual, curled up in the shelter, carefully guarding his treasure between his claws, while Hayex reclined next to his companion.

[111] Meaning *Good Fire*. A purification rite marking the arrival of the good time and was celebrated on May 1. In the celebration, they would free cattle of disease by passing it over a great bonfire. In Ireland, it is commemorated in honor of the first settlers of the island. (Doctors note).

They were immersed in a deep sleep when the sensitive ears of the dragon alerted them to the strange sounds around them. He opened his eyes. Before him the shape of two shadow Pantesux Dragons came into focus: sinister shadows from the deep forest, with their faces covered with the cowardly facade of a black hood.

"Who are you?" he asked alarmed, as he sat up from the forest bed.

"Keep calm, son. Give us the Chalice, or your friend will pay the price," said one of the evil intruders with a malicious snarl as he dangled Hayex from his feet and pointed his sharp weapon at his throat. Tied and gagged, Hayex was defenseless.

Califax drew his sword to defend his position, but the other dragon pointed his sword at the gargoyle's throat, threatening to cut his head off in one fell swoop.

The young dragon had no other choice but to cease his defense. He slowly reached the Chalice out of the bag. Powerless, with trembling claw, he extended the Chalice to the thief. The other dragon, who had not said a word, extended his claw to grasp it. Califax, in a vain attempt to distract them, deliberately let the Holy Grail fall to the ground. The evil intruders only laughed harder at the plight of their hapless victims.

"That is an old trick, son. Surely Filox taught you better tricks than that one," he said with a caustic outburst of laughter that resonated in the deep of the forest.

He reached down to the cup on the ground, but the moment he picked it up, an enormous lance penetrated the back of the evildoer causing him to fall mortally wounded on his mammoth mug.

One after the other, the arrows zipped danger-ously over the dragons' heads. They ceased their pillaging and they flew behind the trees and bushes to hide. The humans have discovered them!

Bravely, Califax returned to pick up the Chalice and fly to the highest part of the trees amidst a rain of arrows and rocks that he skillfully turned aside with his powerful sword.

A long time passed before the humans tired of the persecution. Califax then went searching for his loyal friend. The dark of the night was almost impenetrable. To light a flame would be suicide with the hostile humans patrolling the area. He waited then, for a signal from the gargoyle.

Hayex tossed back and forth vainly trying to untie himself. He uttered distressing moans under the suffocat-ing gag tied around his head and mouth.

"Shut up, if you do not want to be silenced for-ever!" threatened the intruder, hiding in the weeds, hop-ing to surprise Califax.

Searching for his enemy, the dragon inspected a small part of the forest. When he returned, the gargoyle was gone. He turned to see the brilliant sword of the young dragon at his throat.

"Who are you? Do not you know that this Grail will save our country?" inquired Califax searching his face for signs of patriotism.

Just as he finished questioning the hooded dragon, he was struck in the head causing him lose consciousness. After a few minutes, Califax awoke from his stupor, with-out his sword and without the Chalice. He found himself before another enormous Pantesux dragon, flanked by the first one, and also camouflaged by a black hood.

"I did not really think you could do it, Califax. Your father would be very proud of you. It is too bad, but you will not live to tell of your conquest," he threatened.

"Who are you? What you are doing is an attack against our country. If I do not take the Chalice to Dragonia, the entire *Region of Fire* will be devastated by Helion's wrath," he pleaded his cause.

"When that happens, I will be very far away, my friend. The power of this relic will take me to unimagined heights," he said, looking up the sky.

"What are you going to do? We do not know how it works. It could be very dangerous," he warned.

"I know very well what I must do," he asserted, taking the hood off his head simultaneously with the other dragon.

"¿Crulux? ¿Tradux...?" he exclaimed, dumbstruck, before such a revelation.

"You father ordered me to send Crulux and Dragax to search for you. This was an excellent opportunity to obtain the Chalice," informed the traitor, with cynicism.

"Too bad, none of you will return alive," he said, while he stabbed Crulux who, surprised by that infamy, looked fixedly at the eyes of his aggressor before death overtook.

"You are an assassin, Tradux!" protested Califax, after witnessing the brutal act.

"I am foresighted. Thus, I will not have to share the power of the Chalice with anyone," he asserted, while taking his wineskin out of a bag.

Califax took advantage of that brief moment of his enemy's distraction to grab the deceased Crulux's sword and attack the traitor. The clash of the swords rang through the forest, and the flames of the dragons illuminated the dark celestial vault. In spite of being more agile than Tradux, Califax could not manage to vanquish his experienced opponent. However, the young dragon would not give up.

The dragons moved swiftly and brandished their lethal swords to inflict harm to the other. The used every weapon at their disposal, the blows, the merciless tail swats and the fire breathe. Only the silent light of the stars in the sky witnessed the terrible duel between the two committed saurians.

The battle of these titans would soon come to its end. With a quick turn, followed by a great blow with his tail, Califax managed to disarm his enemy. Finding himself defenseless, he remembered then that Califax's magic sword remained lay in the pasture below. He quickly dove to the ground and armed himself with the fantastic weapon. Tradux confronted his opponent knowing that he had a superior weapon in his claws. After a short exchange, Tradux disarmed Califax by cutting the lesser sword in two. Once again, Califax found himself at the mercy of the traitor.

"I will give you the opportunity to witness my glory," he said with pride. "Later, you can join my cause. Once I have the power, I will fill the Chalice with my blood and you will drink of it to seal our pact. Would you drink of my blood, Califax?" inquired the traitor, with a macabre outburst of laughter.

"Never!" he exclaimed bravely, remembering the horrible nightmare that haunted from the start of his adventure.

Tradux filled the Chalice with wine and drank eagerly spilling a little of its content, while Califax felt a repulsive sensation in his stomach to on having watch that scene. Then, the traitor filled and emptied the cup two more times. Nothing happened. Perhaps, the power of the Chalice was nothing more than a lie, or at best, an unfounded myth.

"It does not work!" he exclaimed furiously, and tossing it away scornfully.

Meanwhile, Califax asked himself what had happened. Why did Tradux feel no change? Then, the traitor began to sense a strange flavor in his mouth. It was a sweet flavor, almost like blood, and trying to wash that repugnant flavor away, he drank directly from the wineskin. An intense heat, which ate away at the dragon's entrails, overcame him. With his claws on his throat, he tried to breath in air, and an intense red light, as an ignominious halo glowed around the beast's body. Califax could barely believe the terrible spectacle before him. He stood at a prudent distance, as if to anticipate the powerful destruction of the saurian. Then, the light intensified until it reached a red hot white, much like the hot coals of a gigantic oven, transforming the macabre contours of the unfortunate traitor until he was consumed to ashes while howling frightful screams of pain. After that terrifying spectacle, all that was left of that animal was a mountain of burnt residue that the breeze softly scattered about the forest of Briton. However, the Chalice remained intact, as if nothing had happened. Minutes later, Hayex, who had remained hidden behind the scrubs, came out dragging himself like a worm, since he was still tied and gagged, and Califax, immediately, untied Hayex. After the experience, the daring adventurers rejoiced of going out alive, not without having felt astonishment at what they had just witnessed.

"What a frightful moment, my friend! Do you think it would be a good idea to take the Chalice to Dragonia?" doubted the gargoyle.

"Perhaps there is some ritual to avoid being devoured by its power. We must to alert Filox of what has happened," he said, picking up the Chalice from the ground.

"I have a better idea," suggested Hayex. "Why do not we ask the Magician before taking it to Dragonia? Perhaps he has an answer to this mystery."

Thus, Califax and Hayex took flight on a southern course, to the river basin of the Dee River, home to the mysterious magician and sovereign to the dark fog of Briton. In spite of the great uncertainty that the Grail caused, after that experience, they would not take any more chances. From now on, they would guard the Chalice day and night until delivering it to the very claws of King Rasux.

The Secret of the Dragon

10

The Power of the Grail

THE INCIPIENT LIGHT OF THE DAWN CARESSED the golden Plains, when the daring adventurers reached the mysterious and enigmatic refuge of the Magician.

After his usual appearance, the dragon and the gargoyle, those who still were not being accustomed to such sleight of hand demonstrations, asked the wise man of the forest.

"Sir: I have the Holy Grail in my claws, but I do not know how to use its power," the dragon informed the Magician.

"Only the sovereign wearing the crown with four points can make use of its power," said the Magician, in a deep voice.

"Who is this sovereign? How will I be able to recognize him?" he inquired humbly.

"His crown is made of courage, restraint, justice and wisdom, and it must be exposed to the light of the solstice," intoned the Magician.

"But, how must he to use the Grail, Sir?" Califax insisted.

"The secret of the Grail will be revealed to that one, with humility and love in his heart, who transmits its power by asking the right question."

After these mysterious words, just as he had appeared, Dee, the Magician, disappeared in a sea of thick fog.

"I hate it when he does that!" exclaimed Hayex. "We still had many questions to ask," he complained bitterly.

"What do you think he meant by *transmits its power by asking the right question*? And who would the sovereign that wears the four-pointed crown be?" asked Califax.

"I do not know. I had no idea that the Grail held a secret, my friend," explained Hayex.

"Perhaps, Filox knows what all this means," he said, taking his chin into his claws.

"What is the solstice?" asked the gargoyle.

"It is the longest day of the year, when summer begins," he explained. "We need to hurry, since according to the prophecy, the sovereign must drink from the Chalice in the solstice. ...*And Helion drank with him, the day that his brilliance shone longer than that of Selion, and the nations were released*," Califax remembered.

They then undertook the trip to Dragonia, with their minds and hearts full of hope. Will the Chalice really be able to save his people? That question tormented Califax during the entire trip back to his home.

For some time now, the green pastures of Briton had announced the arrival of spring, and summer's eve was very close at hand. They hurried to get home before the solstice.

They flew in a northerly direction, toward Oban, bordering the southern portion of Mount Ben Nevis until reaching the northern bank of Loch Ness, where they stopped to take short rest.

A smooth breeze blew across the water of that beautiful lake. Califax watched it and remembered his encounter with his friend Nessux.

"Do you know Nessux?" asked the dragon.

"Who…?" surprised, asked the gargoyle.

"He is a giant species of dragon, who lives with his family here in this lake," he explained.

"I do not know any dragon who lives in this lake, my friend. Are you sure?"

"I had just arrived to Briton when I stopped to drink water close by this place, and then, Nessux came out to greet me," he explained. "Let us wait a moment. Perhaps we will have good luck and I will be able to introduce you to him," he suggested.

"It would be very nice to meet him. I hope so."

The adventurers waited in silence, and the murmur that accompanied the wind softly blew over their faces, overpowering their minds as they breathed in the gift of that majestic natural landscape with all their senses. At that moment, they felt a peace in their hearts that they had not experienced for a very long time. The adventures felt privileged once more, giving thanks for being part of that vast and unique universe.

The time allowed contemplating all that beauty did not last long. The humans, who had gathered in a large group around the lake in search of the day's fish, had surprised them as they basked by the lake. The humans attacked with ruthless ferocity as they repeatedly shouted "*Lucifer! Lucifer!*"

They quickly flew away amidst a storm of lances and stones. Once again they had to escape the treacherous two-legged beings. They jumped in the lake, but various boats full of furious men were waiting there to brutally attack the brave globetrotters.

In the middle of that clamor, Hayex fell, seriously wounded by a lance. The mortal sting of the dart had penetrated his torso very close to his heart and the blood began to flow profusely, dyeing the lake a fatal red color.

Califax, armed with bravery and rage upon seeing his innocent fallen friend, returned to rescue him from the water before he drowned. At that moment, the men had those '*diabolic creatures*' fate within reach of their weapons: hatred inspired as a by-product of their dogmas and prejudices. The men had surrounded them!

Showing his natural powers, Califax changed his color to litmus blue, and threateningly extended his powerful wings while holding the injured body of his dear friend with his front claws. Turning around, he blew out an enormous flame meant to scare away his untiring persecutors, but it was useless. The men were armed with huge shields of iron and copper, and they closed in closer around the expeditionary in a circle. They covered themselves from the tenacious and fiery attacks from the dragon. At such close range to their objective, everything seemed to be over.

The final attack of those men was imminent. Brandishing their sharp swords, they fatally approached the dragon to finish his life and that of his companion. All of a sudden, the boats began to rock dangerously back and fourth and several of the navigators fell resoundingly into the lake.

One after another, fell into the water without explanation for such a strange phenomenon. Some tried to return to their battered boats when an enormous head emerged from the depths. It was Nessux! On having seen that imposing creature, the men fled any way they could. However, shortly before they reached their boats, other enormous creatures with long necks blocked their way. Nessux's children had joined in the rescue of his friends. Their efforts were two-fold: to save their friend and to teach the treacherous human a lesson.

Califax reached the edge of the lake and tried to revive his faithful companion, giving him breath and heat from his nose, but Hayex did not respond. The large amount of blood he had lost left him in a funeral albino color.

"Wake up, my friend, please!" he cried between sobs. This time, Hayex died.

Having driven the men away, Nessux and his offspring reunited around Califax. Sadness and desolation seized those mythological beings. They cried over the death of the gargoyle and over the enormous pain in the young dragon's heart.

"None of this has been worth the trouble. None of it!" he protested to the sky, sending out a dreadful roar of pain that was heard all over the region.

With the inert body of Hayex in his arms, Califax undertook the trip back to the *Region of Fire*. Without stopping to rest, he arrived at Cape Duncansby and lined up with the Orkney Isles.

Absorbed as he was in his deep pain, he did not notice the presence of various Viking ships that, again, adored him as the god Thor. This time he ignored their effusive reverences. He wanted only to get to his destination as soon as possible. Perhaps, Filox would have a miraculous remedy to revive his dear friend. Although, the truth was, he had never witnessed such a miracle for any of his own kind.

The night before the solstice surprised the very tired young dragon as he flew over the middle of the North Sea. The sea was flogged by a fierce storm. Finally, he had no other choice than to stop on one of the Shetland Islands and wait for the storm subside. The seconds became minutes and the minutes, hours, as his desperation grew as the gale worsened.

Clinging to Hayex's body, he spoke to him reminding of his achievements and vicissitudes along their incredible adventure. Not one response of any kind from the gargoyle. Califax could no longer bear his suffering and fury in silence. He swore to return for revenge on those who had perpetrated the death of his dear friend. If possible, he would cause the end of the entire human race. So great was the pain and bitterness, that afflicted the young dragon.

At the break of dawn, Califax awoke with a start. Fatigue and anguish had overcome him, and he had fallen asleep without knowing it in the middle of the storm the night before.

In spite of his not having eaten anything for several hours, he immediately took to flight. Even though it was early, he beat his wings desperately trying to reach the fastest possible speed. Sorrow and anger seemed to inject the necessary strength he needed to reach his goal in the least amount of time.

Some hours later, Califax could make out the long yearned for Faroe Islands, which was home to the *Region of Fire*. His destination was in view and he beat his powerful wings even faster while the midday sun announced the imminent arrival of the summer solstice. Nevertheless, an ominous phenomenon was drawn in the sky above the region: Helion began to hide behind Selion.

Finally, upon reaching Dragonia, he went directly to the chambers of Filox, the teacher, who was, as usual, in his favorite place: The Royal Library of Dragonia. He was reading one of his inseparable papyruses.

With his face grayed from hunger and fatigue, Califax fainted in the claws of his teacher, and Filox, astonished by the dramatic and unexpected appearance of his pupil, took him with difficulty to a stone armchair upholstered with fine mould. He then took Hayex's inert body of from his claws and gave Califax a drink of water in an attempt to revive him from his state of dehydration.

After a few moments, Califax awoke. He alerting his teacher as to the nature of the terrible prophecies and they immediately went to the Royal Observatory.

A Filox's assistant, who was there at the time, gave notice of what some had waited for: the return of Califax. His long-awaited return spread like wildfire throughout the entire city of Dragonia. Finally, it reached the ears of his father Novax.

Without hesitating even one moment, Novax with his wife Darta at his side flew to accompany their brave son, who was found in the immense vault of the observatory.

Califax stood in the center of the observatory, the dome had a large opening where the sun would slowly; signal the arrival of summer, but a strange phenomenon had prevented its appearance. The solstice had begun without having shown the light of Helion.

Panic seized the entire *Region of Fire*; every inhabitant flew out of control in every direction screaming and terrified. The untimely darkness that surprised the dragons seemed to announce the fulfillment of the apocalyptic prophecies.

Restlessness of even the most ferocious dragon became apparent in the observatory. The darkness that wrapped around Dragonia penetrated their very souls. "Helion have mercy on our souls!" cried many of the dragons.

In spite of the confusion and panic, Califax, then took the Grail and poured a little water inside, keeping his characteristic calm. He waited a few minutes and the moon began to reveal the light of the sun.

In the center of the observatory, the young dragon began performing a strange ritual to him and for the rest of the city. King Rasux, Filox and Novax, as well as the rest of the Royal Court, became quiet before Califax's serenity.

"Your power emanates from a man and your power has returned to a man! If your power has not served a man, then, whom does the Holy Grail serve?"[112] he expressed sadly, lifting the cup towards the sun.

After pronouncing those words, he brought the Grail to Hayex, and softly opened the lips of the gargoyle and gave him a sip from that simple cup. The chant from the attendants of that strange ceremony, shouted indignation at the top of their lungs inside the building. Novax, looked at his son with respect and admiration, for the generous actions of his son, and with one gesture, he quieted the entire audience.

A ceremonious silence, that seemed interminable, invaded the observatory, while the audience awaited the unexpected. Then, something incredible happened: Hayex's body began to elevate in middle of a refulgent bluish light, and the gargoyle turned back to his natural brownish color.

A whirlwind of lights invaded the vault before the overwhelmed eyes of the spectators. Hayex turned quickly until his shape was lost inside that intense brilliance that made the light of the sun pale in comparison.

---

[112] According to legend, only this question from a noble hearted gentleman could activate the power of the Grail. (Doctors note).

Califax, with the Grail still in his claws, backed away from that brilliance, and a few minutes later, the lights began to dissipate little by little.

Once the lights had extinguished completely, a miracle was revealed before the incredulous eyes of the witnesses: Hayex, who all his life had been but a simple and innocuous forest creature, persecuted unjustly by men, was transformed into a human; a boy of about 15 years old.

Hayex awoke from his deep sleep, and before him, he found Califax, amazed by that extraordinary event.

"What happened? Where are we, my friend?" he asked, still groggy and looking all around him with surprise.

"Hayex, my friend: Is it really you?" inquired the dragon, still quite astonished.

"Perhaps, do you not recognize me? Of course, it is I!" exclaimed Hayex, confused, before such a peculiar question.

"Look at yourself!" advised Califax.

Hayex had not noticed his profound transformation, and, embarrassed, he complained bitterly about his new appearance.

"I have changed into a man!" he observed, with horror.

"I thought that, the power of the Chalice, would only resurrect you, my friend!" explained the dragon in alarm.

"It had been better leave me dead!" he protested.

The audience in the observatory could not explain or give credit to what their eyes had seen. Complaints from the portion of the Royal Court apposed to Filox raised their voices demanding an explanation of the situation.

"Is this the Chalice that will save us from perdition, Filox?" demanded a voice that came from the back of the building.

"The prophecies are a farce! Far from saving our people, the Chalice will cause our extinction!" cried yet another voice.

"Where is your savior wearing the four-pointed crown, Filox? Will this boy save Dragonia?" said Lusux, incredulous.

"Cannot you see? You have him before your very eyes," expressed Filox, pointing to Califax. "This young dragon left our land with one horn on his head and now he has returned with four. He is the one the prophecies speak of," he explained. "How many dragons like him do you know?"

"And what do you plan to do? Change us in to humans?" protested Rhudex. "If Califax drinks from the Chalice he will turn into one of them and we will lose him forever. Is that what his sweet mother wants? Is that what this Royal Court wants? The mission is a failure. We should destroy the Chalice. It is a threat to our race," he screamed hysterically.

"I should tell you, noble dragons, that part of what Filox has told you it is true, but, another part is not," interrupted King Rasux, while the murmuring became louder after that asseveration. "The prophecies indeed speak of things to come, but, also, they speak of things that have already happened, many centuries ago," he said, beginning his story. "Before the *Region of Fire* existed, two twin cities were built in far away lands. The human inhabitants of these cities lived their lives under moral codes that would offend even the most savage of our species, and I will not speak of them in respect to our illustrious females that are present here, today, in this building," he clarified.

"The unbefitting moral conduct of these humans," continued Rasux, "provoked the wrath of their God, who on repeated occasions reprimanded them and warned them against this kind of behavior. However, they did not take heed to the warnings. That God, who could not find even one just inhabitant in the town, destroyed those cities with fire and they disappeared. Nevertheless, the punishment those men would suffer was not over. According to very ancient texts, even older than any of our Sacred Papyruses, the souls of those men were dammed to these lands to inhabit them, forever, under the skin of a ferocious dragon. This way, that God could be assured that, those disobedient men, would not forget the reason they had been destroyed, but it seems that we have forgotten. It is not your fault," he exempted. "The truth has been carefully obscured for all these years, behind the walls of the Palace," he concluded.[113]

"Do you mean, Rasux, that we were humans before?" Lusux inquired in a state of bewilderment.

"That is truth, my friend."

A scandalous manifestation congregated around that preposterous affirmation. The King was ridiculed and laughed at, labeling him senile and decrepit. How-

---

[113] In this tale, Rasux seems to be referring to the misfortunate destiny of Sodom and Gomorrah. Genesis XIX: 24 (Doctors note).

ever, with the patience that a sovereign must exhibit before his subjects, he signaled Filox to bring that mysterious document to him. A few minutes later, Filox returned with a papyrus, that as Rasux had anticipated, looked very ancient.

One by one, the dragons looked at that incredible document that proved their unexpected origins. Many questioned the authenticity of the parchment and left the observatory in a fury. Nevertheless, the definitive test of that improbable story was in Califax's claws. Therefore, Filox directed attention towards the young dragon.

"That unknown God, the one we call Helion, gave us the opportunity to vindicate ourselves before His eyes. There will not be another Chalice that will return us to our original condition," he warned. "And if you ask, why should we do it? I would tell you this: The Earth and its destiny are in the hands of men, and very soon, there will be so many of them that it will be impossible to contain them. Human nature is very strange and contradictory, and we will only be able to do something for ourselves if we infiltrate their ranks. Perhaps they will let us tell our story and advise them on the terrible consequences of living an empty violent life without moral principals. And if they laugh at our story, we still have our own experience that, in one way or another, will be transmitted," he concluded.

Califax looked at his teacher's eyes that were full of sincerity and wisdom. He looked at his parents for an instant that and their complacent smiles signaled that they would let him make the final decision.

Then, he filled the Grail with clear water and drank of it. Moments later, an aura surrounded his body overwhelming the cave with a golden brilliance, which in spite of being extremely radiant, did not hurt the eyes of the witnesses. When that light dissipated, a good-looking boy revealed himself before the audience. The sovereign of the four-pointed crown had become a man.

Hayex ran to Califax to cover him with the royal cape, and every dragon, skeptical or not, ended up giving credit to those historic prophecies. Eventually, all the dragons in the *Region of Fire* drank from that miraculous cup, and finally making up a community that lived in peace and prospered for a very long time.

After the death of King Rasux, Califax took the scepter and converted the *Region of Fire* into the *Farox Islands*, and Dragonia into *Danmarx,*[114]unifying all the tribes of the islands under his wise and indulgent authority. However, the Vikings ended up invading those lands and the battles where inevitable.

Califax, who risked his life to avoid the destruction of his country, was now caught before the hostile presence of the conquerors. Nevertheless, with the calm and patience that characterized his nature, he used every means in order to compromise with the barbarian invaders. However, all his efforts were in vain. Offering a valiant battle alongside his father, Califax, finally, died overcome by the treacherous and indecipherable labyrinth of war.

After the death of his close friend, Hayex returned to Jerusalem to fulfill his promise to the teacher

---

[114] Probably, from these words, derived *The Faroe Islands* and *Denmark*, respectively (Doctors note).

Solomon, who was the first to hear his story. Years later Hayex died a natural death. In spite of his skepticism, the teacher documented the story, but it was not disclosed and it remained a mystery for many years in the Sacred City of Jerusalem.

In the XII century, Richard I, the Lion-Heart, came in the Third Crusade to retake the Sacred City of Jerusalem from the Saracen leader, Saladin. This constituted a new and more brutal Dragonia lasts to present day.

Isaiah, disciple in charge of the Flavius Josephus School at the time Solomon belonged to it, he took most of the documents that had accumulated over the centuries at the academy. Even though the Muslim sovereign allowed access to the city for everyone, Isaiah fled from Jerusalem crossing the desert and confronting many dangers. Tired and downhearted he arrived at Qumran[115] and managed to hide many documents in several caves close to the Dead Sea in Palestine.

The slaughter in Acre and the untiring siege of Richard I, the Lion-Heart, in the Sacred land, obligated Isaiah to flee again from his beloved country and travel to Egypt, taking with him some documents, among them, the papyruses that tell this very story.

He crossed the Red Sea in order to reach Naj' Hammadí,[116] where he hide some other scrolls. From there, he went south, crossing the Nile, to the city of Tebas, into the Valley of Kings, where he was surprised by a frightful sand storm.

[115] Also called Khirbet Qumran. (Rock Ruins) The place where the Dead Sea Scrolls were found in 1947. (Doctors note).
[116] A place where 52 Coptic Gnostic papyri were found in 1945, they were dated as 4th century and included the gospel of Saint Thomas. (Doctors note).

Looking for a refuge to protect himself, Isaiah found a small cavity to hide the last papyruses inside a small vessel. This storm and subsequent storms, managed to seal the hiding place. A short time after having hidden the last scroll, thirst and hunger took the life of Isaiah without he ever knowing that the place where he hide the appreciable papyruses was, in reality, neither more nor less than the access to the tomb of the King Tutankhamen.

The Holy Grail was lost in the middle of the wars and nobody ever saw it again. Many people think that it was rescued by the Knights Templar, from the hands of the barbarians, and taken to France in the XIV century. Later, the Knights Templars fled Scotland to escape the intransigent torment of King Philip IV, whose intentions were to be done with the Order of the Knights Templars and to seize the treasure of them to finance wars. He persecuted them, even before the opposition of Pope Clement V, who had accused the Knights of heresy.

Carrying the legendary treasure, the famous quixotic people crossed the River Seine and managed to reach the Atlantic Ocean, to keep it hidden even to this day in some safe and secret place.

However, the legend of the Holy Grail goes beyond a mythical piece of olive wood. It reminds us that, in our minds, we have the foundations to discover our authentic and universal origins, and that in our hearts we hold a cup where love for ourselves and our fellow man grows, just as Jesus gave us the love we needed for our salvation and in this way converted all of us into Noblemen of His Holy Grail.

The incessant fires that we have breathed on one another over the centuries, have been fed by small religious and cultural differences, that are but the colors of the rainbow that make up human creativity.

The message from the prophets is singular and universal, and lives in the fact that all of us conform to a single race created by an odd act of love, by an All-powerful Entity. And although people call him by different names, He has always been one, and the same, guiding us at all times throughout of short existence.

The bloody battles that we have waged over time in sacred cities and places, in all reality constitute an insult against God, by pretending to take part in them in the name of one religion or another, as if He was not the creator of all men on Earth.

The bonds between nations cannot continue to be based on the use of force without it pushing us, inevitably, to our own total destruction.

Releasing our true human essence and doing away with the indomitable dragon that each one of us carries in our hearts, will lead us, one day, to the peace that we have all yearned for throughout our history.

My name is Charles Halifax, I hold a doctorate in History and I am a descendent in the ancestry of Califax.

The End

The Secret of the Dragon

Author Bio

Carl Cupper, author of *The Secret of the Dragon*, began his courtship of the literary world at the tender age of 40. Cupper, eldest of four brothers, weaves his love of history, philosophy, religion, science, arts and sociology into each of his works of fiction. To date, Cupper's accomplishments include: *Paul and the Cactus; To Live Dieing, to Die Living;* and, *Siege.*

Carl Cupper consistently portrays the restlessness of the human spirit in everything he writes. He depicts the daily turmoil that we perpetuate upon ourselves when we choose to deny to others that which we require for ourselves. Cupper invites us to reflect on the errors of our past, and to apply reasoning and tolerance in our daily lives. He entreats us, in an entertaining way, to accept the responsibility to ensure that each individual has that right to look, to believe and to live in a way that is different from our own.

www.carlcupper.com
carl@carlcupper.com